the evil twin

Cherie Bennett
and
Jeff Gottesfeld

BERKLEY BOOKS, NEW YORK

TRASH: THE EVIL TWIN

A Berkley Book / published by arrangement with
the authors

PRINTING HISTORY
Berkley edition / November 1997

The Putnam Berkley World Wide Web site address is
http://www.berkley.com

ISBN: 0-425-16087-4

BERKLEY®
Berkley Books are published by The Berkley Publishing Group, a member
of Penguin Putnam Inc.,
200 Madison Avenue, New York, New York 10016.
BERKLEY and the "B" design
are trademarks belonging to Berkley Publishing Corporation.

PRINTED IN THE UNITED STATES OF AMERICA

10   9   8   7   6   5   4   3   2   1

Meet the TRASH staff!

the interns

Chelsea—A brainy **Alicia Silverstone** type with a southern twang, she's shocked by the tell-all topics of *Trash*. But by summer's end, *Trash* could be telling Chelsea's big secret!

Karma—This Asian beauty is a downtown Manhattan diva with **Fran Drescher**'s voice. Late nights? Cool clubs? Great shopping? Money to be made? Call Karma!

Lisha—Oh-so-cool, hotter than **Demi Moore**, they call her "Luscious Lisha" on the *Trash* set. She's not the same fat, awkward girl that Chelsea grew up with . . . is she?

Sky—Sweet, laid back, a T-shirt and jeans kind of guy who's a whiz with a movie camera, he gets mistaken a lot on the street for **Keanu Reeves** and is everyone's best bud.

Alan—This sensitive writer from Texas is sure the trash on *Trash* will give him tons of material. If **Johnny Depp** were a writer, he'd be Alan!

Nick—A Canadian slacker with a heart of gold. Chelsea's madly in love with this **Brad Pitt** double, but she has to wait in line behind their famous boss, Jazz Stewart!

continued . . .

the bosses

Jazz—The gorgeous **Daryl Hannah**–ish host of *Trash* is afraid of nothing, whether it's posing for nude pix on the beach in France, riding her Harley onto the set while clad in a bikini, or having three boyfriends at once. Because it's all *Trash,* isn't it?

Roxanne—The beautiful, icy, and ambitious associate producer, she's **Sharon Stone** at age twenty-something, and loathes all interns on principle! Behind her back, they call her "Bigfoot" . . . after those gigantic size-twelve dawgs!

Barry—The slick producer with the power, he's willing to help Chelsea go big places at *Trash.* The question is, is she willing to pay his price?

Sumtimes—Can a girl have a shaved head and still be gorgeous? Yes! The interns' fave producer got her nickname because she sometimes calls herself Cindy, sometimes Julia, sometimes *whatever*!

TRASH:
it's not just a job, it's an adventure!

For Stanley Brechner and
the American Jewish Theatre, New York, NY

They rock.

What did that girl just say?

The thought didn't just flash into Karma Kushner's brain. It flashed through her whole diminutive, five-foot-tall, size two, eighteen-year-old body.

Karma had been momentarily distracted by a backstage noise while her friend Chelsea escorted the last guest onto the set of *Trash,* the highest-rated, most outrageous talk show in the history of talk shows. Today's topic was "Teen Kids of Mass Murderers," and the show was almost over.

But Karma and her two best friends and roommates, Lisha Bishop and Chelsea Jennings, had good reason to dread this last part of the show.

It had to do with Chelsea's dirty, big secret.

Karma knew who the guest, an attractive teen girl, was *pretending* to be, but she had no

1

idea who the guest really *was*.

She's pretending to be Chelsea Kettering, teen daughter of famous mass murderer Charles Kettering, Karma thought. *But she can't possibly be the real Chelsea Kettering, because only Lisha and I know who that really is, and—*

"My name is Liza Campbell," the Chelsea Kettering impostor announced as the cameras came in close, "and I am definitely not Chelsea Kettering."

"No?" Jazz Stewart, the gorgeous, hot, nineteen-year-old host of *Trash* asked innocently.

"No," Liza repeated. "Here she is." Liza smiled at Jazz.

Here who is? Karma thought. And then she realized what was about to happen, and a sick feeling of dread filled her stomach. *Oh, no . . .*

A rolling camera closed in on Chelsea Jennings, until it was right in her face, up close and personal. Chelsea's Alicia Silverstone good looks were being beamed live to television sets across North America and around the world.

Jazz found out the truth, Karma guessed. *She knows that Chelsea Jennings is the real Chelsea Kettering, and she's about to out her on national television.*

Karma glanced quickly to her left, where her other best friend, Lisha Bishop, was standing. Lisha had a look of raw shock on her face, a look that matched Chelsea's on the monitors.

Chelsea seemed frozen to the spot, unable to

2

move. All she could do was look into the camera and realize that her terrible secret, the secret she had not even told her boyfriend, Nick Shaw, was about to be exposed to the entire world on national television.

This is the second time Chelsea's face is being broadcast on TV to the whole world, Karma thought. *But the last time she was a hero. This time, she's no hero. This time—*

"Here's the girl you're looking for, Jazz," Liza announced dramatically, giving Chelsea a smug look.

Chelsea had been assigned to walk the girl out onto the set, and so at the moment she was standing not five feet from her. Liza took a step, lifted her arm, and pointed directly at Chelsea. "This is Charles Kettering's real daughter! This is Chelsea Kettering!"

The audience went wild. It was pandemonium. Everyone was talking at once, yelling, screaming, applauding.

"This is the real Chelsea Kettering," Liza said again, when the audience was quieted. It was hanging on her every word. "She calls herself Chelsea Jennings," she continued, "but her real name is Chelsea Kettering. The Burger Barn shooter in Johnson City, Tennessee, who killed all those people, was her father. She's been living a secret life all these years—"

"Imagine," Jazz cooed, "the most famous teen kid of a mass murderer was our little intern Chelsea all this time!"

"Oh—my—gawd," Karma muttered out loud to herself in her trademark Long Island whine, "I can't believe Jazz did this." All she could do was stand there in the wings and watch as Jazz turned Chelsea's dark secret into a public nightmare.

"It's not such a secret now," Jazz continued, smiling for the cameras. "Is it, Chelsea?"

Karma and Lisha traded looks of horror and shrugged helplessly at each other from across the stage.

Chelsea just stood there, mute, like a deer caught in some oncoming car's headlights.

"When we come back," Jazz continued, flipping her long, blond hair over her shoulders, "we'll have a little *tête-à-tête* with Chelsea Jenn—ah, I mean, Chelsea *Kettering,* who just happens to be one of our six teen interns right here on *Trash.* Cool, huh?"

"Gang," Jazz told the live studio audience, "it doesn't get any *trashier* than this."

And then she used an expression she'd been starting to use more and more frequently on the show, as sort of a trademark for herself—as if Jazz Stewart needed any more trademarks.

"How trashy it is!"

The *Trash* studio audience echoed Jazz. *"How trashy it is!"* they all yelled. Then they went wild with cheering and applause, and this time, they were unprompted by any flashing "applause" signs or show personnel urging them to

4

be demonstrative. This was a wholly sponta-
neous celebration.

Trash, and its nineteen-year-old host, Jazz
Stewart, recently named by two national maga-
zines as the "Sexiest Woman in America," had
just pulled off the publicity coup of the year.
Again.

The show went to commercial break—Karma
knew the schedule for the "Teen Kids of Mass
Murderers" show practically by heart. And she
knew that they had just four minutes before the
show would come back, live on the air.

She couldn't help herself.

She ran out onto the set, over to her friend,
who still stood there, next to Jazz, immobilized
with fear.

Out of the corner of her left eye, she could see
Lisha running out onto the set, too.

And out of the corner of her right eye, she
could see the girls' nemesis, *Trash* producer
Roxanne Renault, standing with her arms
crossed, a sneering, self-satisfied grin on her
gorgeous Sharon Stone look-alike face.

"Chels?" Karma asked, reaching her friend at
the same time that Lisha did.

"Kushner! Bishop!" Roxanne hissed from the
wings. "Get the hell off my set!"

Karma ignored Roxanne as Chelsea turned to
her.

"Chels, are you okay?"

Chelsea nodded blankly.

"Look, you don't have to let them get away

5

with this," Lisha said quickly. "You can just turn around right now and walk off this set."

"Don't even think about it, Chelsea," Jazz said sweetly. "You wreck my show and I'll wreck your life."

"You've already wrecked her life!" Lisha retorted, reaching for her friend. "Come on, Chels—"

Karma and Lisha put their arms around their friend to lead her offstage before the commercial break came to an end.

"I'm staying," Chelsea mumbled, her eyes blank.

"But, Chelsea, that's nuts," Karma protested.

"What difference could it possibly make now?" Chelsea asked, her eyes still blank and glassy. "The whole world knows now."

"One minute," the assistant stage manager called.

"Kushner and Bishop," Roxanne yelled again from the wings, "you will get off that stage now or you're both fired!"

Karma thought quickly. "Listen, Chels," she advised, reaching again for her friend's arm, "don't volunteer any information. I'll find you a lawyer. You can probably sue *Trash* for—"

"You know, Karma, I like your spirit," Jazz said, laughing. "You don't know squat, of course, but I do like your spirit."

"Thirty seconds!" the assistant called.

"Please, Chelsea, you don't have to stay out here—" Lisha began.

"Get off my stage!" Roxanne, also known to the interns as Bigfoot because of the huge size of her feet, hissed to Lisha and Karma. "Now!"

Karma gave Chelsea's hand a quick squeeze before she let go. "You'll be okay."

"I'll never be okay again," Chelsea said, still staring, still glassy-eyed.

Karma and Lisha hurried to the wings, deliberately choosing the opposite side of the stage from where Roxanne was standing.

"I can't believe this is happening," Karma moaned. "I feel like it's my fault."

"Because it is," Lisha told her, folding her arms around her body and watching Chelsea anxiously.

"You didn't need to agree with me so quickly," Karma whined.

"You got her into this mess—"

"All I did was try to help Chelsea keep her secret by getting some friend of my stockbroker's in Australia to pretend she was Chelsea Kettering!" Karma protested.

"What I want to know is how the hell they found out the truth about Chelsea," Lisha muttered.

"Me, too," Karma agreed. "This sucks in a major fashion."

"Ten seconds," the assistant called. "Nine, eight, seven . . ."

"Good luck, Chelsea," Karma murmured, even though she knew her friend couldn't hear her.

"I wish we could help her." Lisha was tight-lipped, her eyes on Chelsea.

"Four and . . ." The techie pointed to Jazz, who smiled into Camera One.

"We're back," she said. "And my special guest is Chelsea Kettering, teen daughter of mass murderer Charles Kettering." Jazz smiled at Chelsea, who still looked shell-shocked.

"So, Chelsea," Jazz continued, "obviously you lied to the whole world about who you are. I mean, you lied to me, your employer here at *Trash*. Which was an utterly trashy thing to do, I might add."

Chelsea was mute.

"What I'd like to know, Chelsea, is, what's it like to know that your father killed so many people? And what's it like to know that right before your mother murdered him, the last person he was trying to kill was . . . you?"

Karma got into the elevator of her apartment building and pushed the button for her floor.

What a day, she thought, leaning her head back against the wall of the elevator.

"Well, you wanted a more exciting life than you had on Long Island," she told herself, aloud. "You wanted it, you got it."

My life has changed so much since I got picked over tens of thousands of other applicants to be one of the six summer interns on Trash, she thought. *I got to move into the city, to work on the hottest talk show in TV history, got the five*

greatest new friends in the world, and the great-
est boyfriend on earth.

I never had friends like Lisha and Chelsea be-
fore in my life. We didn't even know each other
before the summer started—I mean, Chelsea
and Lisha were best friends when they were
kids, but Lisha moved away and they didn't see
each other until they met in the apartment a few
weeks ago. But now all three of us are best
friends.

Who would think that I, tiny Karma Kushner,
Korean-American adopted daughter of Jewish
former hippies who own a health-food store on
Long Island, would be best buds with a preppie
brain from Tennessee who looks like Alicia Sil-
verstone, and a Demi Moore look-alike rock-and-
roller from Colorado who spent a year in Eu-
rope.

It's not just the three of us, either. There's
Nick, and Sky, and Alan, the guy interns, who
live right across the hall from us. Nick and
Chelsea are a hot couple. What's Nick going to
say about this? How's he going to feel when he
finds out that Chelsea never told him who she
really is?

Probably about as good as Chelsea feels know-
ing that Jazz is pregnant and Nick might be the
father, Karma thought ruefully.

Now, my guy, Demetrius Raines—or Mr.
Studly, as he is affectionately called at Trash—
would never pull something like that.

I hope.

9

I guess the big question is, what's going to happen now?

Karma got out of the elevator and went to her front door, where she unlocked the three locks. Lisha was sitting on the sofa with the TV on, the remote control in her hand.

"Chelsea here?" Karma asked. It was nearly ten o'clock that night, and she had just left the *Trash* offices. Roxanne had insisted she stay late to transcribe endless tapes from crazed fans who wanted to leave messages on the 900-number by dialing 1-900-I'M TRASH.

"Nick took her to a friend's place in Queens for the night," Lisha reported. "She wants to stay away from reporters for a while."

"So why isn't the phone ringing off the hook?" Karma asked, getting a Coke from the fridge.

"Because I was smart enough to unplug it," Lisha answered. "Are there any reporters downstairs?"

"Only a few," Karma said. "I guess they figured out that Chelsea never came back here today."

"They're vultures," Lisha said bluntly. She reached into a bag of Hershey Kisses, unwrapped one, and popped it into her mouth. "It's the same zoo as last time. Only worse."

"How much worse?" Karma asked.

"Look at this." As Lisha spoke she pressed the volume switch on the remote.

Kate Pride, a well-known anchorwoman who

10

now also had her own people-oriented news show, filled the screen.

"Teen talk-show host Jazz Stewart has done it again," Pride announced. "A few weeks ago on her show, *Trash* summer intern Chelsea Jennings saved the day with her quick thinking live on the air."

Behind Pride, a video clip of the Sela Flynn incident on *Trash* could be seen.

"Today, *Trash* pulled a surprise coup, when the viewing public got to see who Chelsea Jennings really is."

The video changed to a close-up of Chelsea.

"Oh no," Lisha groaned.

"Oh yes." Karma sighed.

"It turns out that Chelsea Jennings is not really her name at all," Kate Pride said. "Her real name is Chelsea Kettering. And she is the daughter of Charles Kettering. You may recall that Charles Kettering was a prominent attorney in Johnson City, Tennessee, who went berserk one day and entered a Burger Barn restaurant, where he shot and killed every single patron and worker in sight. Then he went home to kill his wife and baby daughter. But before he could kill the baby, his wife stabbed him to death with a kitchen knife.

"That baby," Kate continued, "grew up to be Chelsea Kettering. Or, as we all knew her, Chelsea Jennings. Even *Trash* couldn't make up a story quite this . . . well, trashy."

Pride's voice-over continued as the television

11

footage shifted to news footage from the day of the Burger Barn shooting incident—people being taken out of the Burger Barn on stretchers, Chelsea's family's nice house in a rich section of Johnson City, shots of the shattered plate glass of the Burger Barn, dozens of police cars and SWAT-team vehicles.

Again, the close-up of their best friend.

"We have here in our studio famous pop-culture expert, Grace Caramelcorn, to discuss the implications of this news-breaking story. Welcome, Grace."

The camera went to an aggressively thin woman in her thirties with perfectly bleached-blond hair. "Thank you, Kate."

"Grace, today, on her top-rated, outrageous teen TV talk show, *Trash,* Jazz Stewart again proved why she has no equal in the pop-culture business."

"I'd have to agree with you, Kate," Grace said.

"Let's watch some footage from today's segment together," Kate went on, "and then I'd like to ask you what you think this says about our society at the end of the twentieth century."

Now the footage shifted, to a segment from this afternoon's *Trash.*

"I don't want to watch this again," Karma whined.

"I do," Lisha insisted. "I can't believe how Chelsea—"

There was a close-up of Jazz, and then her voice cut Lisha's off.

"So, Chelsea," Jazz said, "how did you manage to keep it such a secret all these years that you're Kettering's kid?"

Chelsea, on the TV screen, looked right at Jazz. "I never told anyone," she said simply.

"But surely you had a need to let the truth out," Jazz said, feigning sympathy.

"Not really," Chelsea answered. Her gaze had changed from shell-shocked to steady, and her eyes met Jazz's. "But it doesn't look like I have much of a choice, now, do I?"

"You go, girl!" Karma cheered.

"What about your mother?" Jazz pressed. "Where's she?"

"None of your business," Chelsea answered. "Although I bet you'll figure it out soon enough, if in fact you don't have that information already."

Jazz smiled at Chelsea. "Maybe we do," she said sweetly. "So, I'm very curious, Chelsea. Do you have any of your father's murderous rages?"

"Why, yes, Jazz," Chelsea replied. "I do."

Jazz looked surprised at her answer. "Really?"

"Really," Chelsea repeated evenly. "In fact, I'm having one right about . . . now!"

The audience cheered, and the news report went back to Kate Pride's face.

"Ethical or unethical," Pride said to Grace Caramelcorn, "you have to admit it was great

13

live television. But what are the sociological implications of all this?"

"Click it off," Karma pleaded. "This is so disgusting!"

Lisha clicked off the television. "'You have to admit it was great live television,'" Lisha mocked Kate Pride's practiced delivery. "Gimme a break." She stuffed another Hershey's Kiss into her mouth.

Karma reached over and took a handful of chocolates. "I can't stand what Jazz did," she said, "but she is some sort of a sicko genius."

"Sick is the operative word," Lisha said darkly. "And we're going to find a way to get back at her. I know we will."

"Well, you know what my parents would say." Karma unwrapped a chocolate as she talked. "Her karma is seriously bad. Jazz and Bigfoot will both get theirs."

"Yeah, well, if they have to wait 'til their next lifetimes to get zapped for their evil deeds, then I'd just as soon make sure we exact a little justice in this one." She unwrapped the last chocolate in the bag. "Look at this, I'm stuffing my face with chocolate over those two idiots!"

"Chocolate will cure anything," Karma opined. "My parents say that about carrot juice. But then, they are seriously disturbed."

Lisha sucked on the candy. "Did Roxanne ever tell you how they figured it out?"

"That our Chelsea is really Chelsea Kettering?" Karma asked. "I have no idea. I was totally sure they were clueless."

"Well, they're not." Lisha sounded disgusted. "That's obvious."

Karma drained her Coke and got up to throw the can into the garbage. "We'll find out soon."

"How do you know?"

"Because," Karma said, slipping out of her high heels, "Bigfoot sent me and Chelsea an interoffice memo. We're supposed to be in her office first thing in the morning."

"You think she's going to fire you?" Lisha asked.

"That would be stupid," Karma said. "I heard the flash ratings came in and today's show was second only to the Sela Flynn hostage show. And, as you know, that show beat the O.J. verdict!"

"So then, what's up, do you think?" Lisha asked.

Karma shrugged. "I have to admit, I have no idea."

The intercom buzzer rang. Lisha went to the box and spoke into it. "Yeah, Antoine?"

Antoine was their doorman. He had a serious problem with leaving work to go play the trotters, but for once he was actually on duty.

All that came back to Karma was static.

"Yeah, sure," she said cheerfully.

"You have no idea who you just said could come up," Lisha pointed out. "You used to be so careful."

"I know." Karma sighed. "I've become a real New Yorker. I open my door to mass murderers. Oops. I guess that wasn't funny."

There was a knock on the door. Karma peered through the peephole, then happily and quickly undid the locks and jumped into her boyfriend's arms.

"Demetrius!" she cried.

He was so huge that she hung suspended in the air.

"You're very cute," he told her, grinning down at her.

"The cutest," she agreed as he set her down. "Come on in."

"I should have called first, I know," Demetrius said quickly as he came in and sat in the overstuffed chair. "But I was at a diner over on Broadway with my brother, and I just took a chance that you were here."

"I'm here." Karma sat herself in his lap, her legs over the arms of the chair, her arms wrapped around his muscular neck.

"Very here," Demetrius said, laughing. "I knew you'd be really upset about what happened with Chelsea today. I was so busy I didn't even get to see you. I wanted to make sure that you know I knew nothing at all about all of this."

"I never thought you did," Karma assured him. She snuggled close and kissed him tenderly.

"Uh, excuse me, there is a third party in the living room," Lisha reminded Karma.

"Oh, don't worry, all my clothes are staying on," Karma told her. "For the moment, anyway."

"Where's Chelsea?" Demetrius asked.

"Nick took her to a friend's," Karma replied. "Smart, huh?"

"Did he know all this about her?" Demetrius asked.

"No," Karma answered. "She was thinking about telling him. But then, you know, this whole thing happened with Jazz getting pregnant, and then there's all the dish about Jazz and Nick—"

"But Chelsea and Nick are tight again, aren't they?" Demetrius asked, his brow furrowed.

"Yeah." Lisha raised an eyebrow. "So?"

"So," Demetrius replied, "all I have to say is that if the girl I loved kept something that major from me, it would really bother me."

"Relax," Karma whined. "My father owns a health-food store and he wears black socks with sandals. The fashion police may be looking for him, but he's embarrassingly normal."

"So, what are you saying, that if your girlfriend kept something like this from you that you'd break up with her over it?" Lisha asked Demetrius curiously.

"I don't know," he answered. "I might."

Karma turned to him. "You don't think Nick will . . . no, he wouldn't. He couldn't."

Demetrius shrugged. "I just don't know," he

said. "But I think it's possible that their relationship could be in really, really big trouble."

"But look at what Chelsea has put up with from Nick!" Lisha cried.

"Oh-my-gawd," Karma muttered, "I just had the most terrible thought."

"What?" Lisha asked.

"That Jazz really, really wants Nick back. So even if she isn't really pregnant with his kid, this is all part of her plot to break up Nick and Chelsea."

"That's sick," Lisha declared.

"True," Demetrius agreed. "But the really awful thing is, it might just work."

"**S**it down," Bigfoot told Karma and Chelsea.

They sat.

It was the next morning, and as ordered, Karma and Chelsea had shown up at Roxanne's office. Karma had barely had a chance to talk with Chelsea about how she felt, or how Nick was taking everything. There had been a throng of reporters outside *Trash* that morning, and Chelsea had snuck in through the back entrance. They had not said more than "how are you?" and "okay" to each other before hurrying in to this meeting.

"So, Chutney, you are famous once again," Roxanne said, her hands behind her head. Today she was wearing black flared pants with a black jacket that zipped up the front over an orange-sherbet-colored blouse. The material covering her cast matched her skirt.

"Am I supposed to thank you for that?" Chelsea asked coldly.

"You should be thanking me for not firing you when I found out what a liar you are," Roxanne said mildly. "Did the two of you really believe you could outsmart me?"

"Frankly, yes," Karma said.

"I didn't get where I am because of my great looks, you know," Bigfoot said, "although being as good-looking as I am helps when you work in a visually-oriented industry."

"I'll remember that," Karma declared solemnly.

"It was so much fun, really," Bigfoot continued blithely. She looked at Chelsea. "Especially the part where I pretended I didn't believe you when you came in here with your big confession."

"So you already knew then." Chelsea's eyes were cold.

"Aren't we quick," Roxanne said, marveling. "I bet you were just the brightest thing back in Hayseed, Tennessee."

"That's Nashville," Chelsea corrected.

"Whatever," Roxanne said airily. "The truth is, you have a distant cousin—I think we found her in Minnesota, or something, who talked. For a price, of course. Everyone has a price, you know. Once she talked, the rest was easy. We didn't have to go far to find you."

"How did you know that the girl you spoke to

in Australia wasn't really Chelsea Kettering?" Karma asked.

Roxanne gave her a jaded look. "Well, Karma, you made one little error. With the girl in Australia you got to pretend to be Chelsea Kettering, the one I spoke with over the phone. That one. The one who told me she would never even consider coming on *Trash*?"

"Yeah," Karma said warily.

"Well, I told you I wouldn't take no for an answer. I hired an Australian reporter to go visit with this girl and offer her major bucks to come on our show."

"And she told your reporter the truth?" Chelsea guessed.

"Not hardly," Roxanne snorted. "I guess you two never actually met her. In person, I mean."

"I don't understand," Karma said.

Bigfoot leaned over her desk. "She's black."

"Oops," Karma said meekly.

"You girls seriously underestimated both our brains and our resources," Roxanne said smugly. "Which is why we win, and you lose."

"No one was keeping score, Roxanne," Chelsea said evenly.

"Liar." Roxanne laughed. "Everyone keeps score. That's the way the world is."

"Maybe that's the way *your* world is," Chelsea said.

Roxanne laughed again. "You can drop the holier-than-thou act from now on, Chelsea.

After all, I know what kind of people you come from."

Chelsea leaned forward and grabbed the edge of Bigfoot's desk so hard that her fingers turned white and bloodless. "Look, if you're going to fire me, just fire me. But I never, and I mean never, want to hear you say one thing about my family or anyone in it ever again. Is that clear?"

Roxanne looked amused. "Why, Chelsea, I do believe I hit a nerve. And what makes you think you can threaten me?"

Chelsea stood up. "Because right now I'm a star. And I can go to the media and tell them anything I want to tell them about you, or Jazz, or *Trash,* and the whole world will listen."

Now Chelsea leaned over Bigfoot's desk, and she looked her dead in the eye. "So don't mess with me. And now this meeting is over."

"I can't believe you did that!" Karma was exhilarated. "I mean, I was there, I heard you, but I still can't believe you told Bigfoot off and then ended the meeting! I wish I had the whole thing on video!"

It was that evening, and Karma, Demetrius, Nick, and Chelsea were out in Brooklyn at Nick's friend's apartment. The friend was an actor, and he was on location in North Carolina shooting a commercial.

Karma had just finished relating to Nick and Demetrius what Chelsea had said to Roxanne that morning. When the meeting was over, Roxanne had basically left Chelsea alone. Jazz, however, had insisted that Chelsea be present at a news conference in the afternoon. Jazz had planned to answer all the questions and just have Chelsea stand there, looking helpless. Unfortunately for Jazz, though, the reporters all wanted to talk to Chelsea, and not to Jazz, so Jazz had quickly cut the news conference short.

After that, the gang had managed to get Chelsea out of the *Trash* offices by putting her in a trash bin and having the janitor carry her out with the garbage. She had the key to Nick's friend's apartment, and as planned, they had all met her there after work.

"It's really beautiful," Nick said. "They can't fire either of you now. Chelsea is too famous."

"Well, they could fire me," Karma informed him.

"But they won't," Demetrius said firmly. "They love all the publicity."

"I'm really hungry, you guys," Karma declared. "Want to order Chinese?"

They all agreed.

"I'll call from the bedroom." Demetrius got up from the chair he was sitting in. "I know a great place near here."

"How do you know a great Chinese restaurant in this part of Brooklyn?" Karma asked curiously.

"Mindy Moscow lives right around the corner," Demetrius explained.

"Oh," was all Karma said. Mindy Moscow was Demetrius' last girlfriend. She had been his first love, and they had had a very serious, long-term relationship.

And she's this incredibly hot alternative singer, Karma recalled miserably, *who looks like a tall Kate Moss, only with breasts. She has a huge cult following. In fact, I'm pretty sure I read recently that a bunch of record labels all want to sign her.*

Yeah. Like I can compete with that. Not that I'd ever let on to Demetrius that I ever feel insecure. That is just not my style.

"I'll go with you," Karma offered, scrambling up from the rug where she'd been sitting. "You never order enough food."

Karma sat on the bed with Demetrius while he ordered.

"And extra sesame noodles," she told him. "Oh, and I want three egg rolls."

Demetrius finished ordering and hung up the phone. He turned to Karma. "Where do you put it?"

"I love Chinese food," she said with a shrug. She lay down on her side and propped her head up by leaning on one elbow. "So, you and Mindy used to hang around here, huh?"

Demetrius nodded. He lay down on his side facing her. "It's a nice neighborhood. Very family-oriented."

Karma rolled over onto her back and stared up at the ceiling. "So, do you ever hear from Mindy?" she asked casually.

He leaned over her, an impish grin on his face. "Why?"

"Just curious," she said easily, staring up at the ceiling. "Have you ever noticed how many ceilings look like cottage cheese?"

Demetrius laughed, leaned over, and kissed her. "You really *are* hungry!"

"But not for—gag me—cottage cheese," Karma said with a shudder. "Way too healthy."

Softly, Demetrius kissed her again. "You know, you're a very beautiful girl," he said softly.

"Yeah, I know," Karma whined. "And it's quite a cross to bear. Or, in my case, quite a star of David. That's a joke," she added.

Demetrius laughed. "I know it's a joke, you nut." He looked thoughtful for a moment. "It's funny, isn't it? I've only had two serious girlfriends in my life, and they're both Jewish. Pretty ironic for a Greek-Hispanic American like me."

"You and I are both just so exotic," Karma teased. "And you can imagine how the Jewish guys are all over me. I mean, here I am, both Asian chic and a nice, Jewish girl they can take home to their mother!"

Demetrius laughed. "I'll have to take you home to my mother sometime. She'll love you."

Karma twirled a lock of Demetrius' long hair around her finger. "Did you ever take Mindy?"

"Where?"

"Home to meet your mother," Karma elaborated.

"Yeah, she met my parents," Demetrius said. "They thought she was great. You would, too."

"Yeah? I'd love to meet her sometime," Karma lied. "I hear she's a really great singer. I'd love to hear her."

"She said she'd love to meet you, too."

"She did?" Karma asked in surprise. "When?"

"When I talked to her on the phone last week and told her about you," he explained. "Hey! I just thought of something!"

"What?"

"When I talked to Mindy she mentioned that she was singing tonight at Molten Java. It's a new club. We should go!"

"What, tonight?" Karma asked, taken aback.

"Sure. Why not?"

"Well, because Chelsea is, like, reeling from the major turn of events in her life," she said, thinking quickly. "And people would recognize her."

"So we'll disguise her or something," Demetrius said. He pulled Karma up. "Come on, let's go ask them if they want to go."

"Who said I want to go?" Karma asked.

"You did."

"No, I didn't."

"You said you wanted to meet her and you

wanted to hear her sing." Demetrius looked baffled.

"I didn't mean *tonight*!"

"Come on, it'll be fun! And she won't be singing in little clubs much longer," he added. "She's about to sign with Warner Brothers."

"Lucky her."

"Let's go ask Chelsea and Nick," Demetrius said enthusiastically. He hurried into the living room, Karma trailing behind him. Chelsea had her head in Nick's lap. He was stroking her hair. Demetrius quickly made his proposal.

"But you guys don't want to go, of course," Karma said quickly. "It would be a nightmare for you, Chels."

Chelsea sat up. "Maybe I could wear a disguise or something."

"That's just what I said!" Demetrius agreed.

"But . . . but we should stay here and . . . and plan," Karma improvised.

They all looked at her.

"Plan what?" Nick asked.

"Chelsea's future," she said quickly.

"That is the very last thing I want to do," Chelsea said, getting up from the couch.

Nick got up, too. "Come on," he told her, taking her hand. "I know where Billy keeps all his crazy Halloween costumes. The guy's a total pack rat. We'll find you a great disguise, then we'll go out and have fun."

"And forget all this stuff with *Trash* ever

happened," Chelsea agreed. "At least for a few hours."

Hand in hand, they went into the tiny second bedroom where Billy O'Reilly, Nick's friend, kept all his stuff.

"This is great," Demetrius said cheerfully. "It's going to be a blast."

"Oh, yeah," Karma agreed, trying to look happy.

Demetrius went to her. "You're okay with this, aren't you?"

"Sure," Karma declared. "Why wouldn't I be okay? You and Mindy are still friends, I take it."

"Good friends," Demetrius confirmed.

"Like, how good?" she asked carefully.

"Well, I care about her," he said. "Just because we broke up doesn't mean I stopped caring."

"I thought when couples broke up they were supposed to hate each other's guts afterward," Karma said.

"Why?" Demetrius asked. "Is that what happened to you?"

"Nothing ever happens to me," Karma commented in her usual honest manner. "I never dated a gorgeous, famous person. Well, there was the time that David Bowie was, like, dying for me—"

"You're a very funny girl." Demetrius smiled.

"Yeah, so I hear." Smirking, Karma plopped down on the couch.

He sat next to her. "You're not . . . jealous, are you?"

Karma laughed, a little too heartily. "Me? Jealous?" She laughed again.

"I didn't think so." Demetrius put his arm around her. "I really love that you're so self-confident, you know?"

"Oh, sure," Karma said breezily. "It doesn't bother me that you're so gorgeous that girls you've never seen before hand you their phone numbers when we're out on a date together."

"That only happened once," Demetrius protested, blushing.

"Twice," Karma corrected. "But, hey, no prob here. So you're, like, this Greek-god studly type. I already knew that."

Demetrius looked uncomfortable. "I sure don't think of myself that way at all."

"Yeah, me, neither," Karma agreed, deadpan. "I love you for your inner beauty."

He leaned over and kissed her. Softly, then passionately. They were lost in each other until the insistent sound of the intercom buzzer interrupted them.

"Ignore it," Karma told him when he tried to get up to answer it.

"But it's dinner," Demetrius reminded her. He went to the door and buzzed the delivery in.

"Mmmmm, I smell food," Nick said appreciatively, coming back into the living room with Chelsea.

"Dig in," Demetrius invited, laying it all out on the coffee table in front of the couch.

"How much do I owe you?" Nick asked.

"It's on me." Demetrius handed Karma an egg roll.

"So, did you guys find a disguise for Chelsea?" Karma asked, biting into the steaming egg roll.

Chelsea blushed. "We forgot to look."

Karma laughed. "So what were you doing in there all that time, as if I didn't know?"

"Probably the same thing you two were doing out here," Nick said easily, grabbing a pair of chopsticks.

The four of them ate happily for a few minutes.

"Y'all, this is great," Chelsea finally said. "I mean, it's really nice of you to hang out—or I guess I should say *hide* out—here with me." She stabbed a prawn and popped it into her mouth.

"If we go out and people recognize you, it'll be a zoo," Karma pointed out.

"You're right." Chelsea nodded. "Maybe we really should just stay right here."

Nick looked up from his plate. "You sure that's what you want to do?"

"I think so."

"Then you got it." He leaned over to kiss her, then turned to Demetrius. "You guys could still go—"

"Oh no," Karma said quickly. "We're here for Chelsea. Right, Demetrius?"

"Right," Demetrius agreed. "The four of us can go hear Mindy sing another time. She's going to be at the Bottom Line in a few days—"

"You must be a big fan to know her performance schedule so well," Nick commented.

Demetrius took a second helping of fried rice. "She used to be my girlfriend."

"For real?" Nick asked. "Hey, I heard her sing in Toronto last year. She's really great!"

"Yeah, she is," Demetrius agreed.

"And she's gorgeous," Nick added.

"Yeah," Demetrius agreed again.

"Talented, semi-famous, and gorgeous," Karma quipped. "God, her life must suck, huh?"

"Talented, semi-famous, and gorgeous applies to Chelsea, too," Demetrius pointed out.

Chelsea sighed. "I am hardly gorgeous. And I never wanted to be famous. Certainly not like this." She put her fork down.

"It won't last," Nick predicted. "Next week the world will move on to a different scandal."

"Chels," Karma asked, "have you called your mom yet?"

"Once this afternoon," Chelsea replied. "The answering machine was on. I left the phone number here. But she hasn't called, so maybe the bloodsuckers never found her."

"Oh, come on," Karma chided. "It's not difficult."

Chelsea bit at her lower lip. "The truth is, I really don't want to talk to her. I feel like this is all her fault."

"How's that?" Demetrius asked.

"Because all these years she made me feel like I had to keep this big, dirty secret about who we really are. It made me feel as if I'd done something wrong."

"But you were just a little baby!" Karma exclaimed.

"I know that logically," Chelsea said, nervously twisting a lock of her hair. "You'd have to know my mother. She just . . . pretends we're this happy, normal family."

"Wishful thinking, maybe," Nick guessed.

"She would never talk about the truth with me." Chelsea's expression was sad as she looked over at Nick. "That's why it was so hard for me to tell you. My mother made me feel like I was . . . dirty, or something."

"There is a therapist's couch somewhere with your name on it," Karma declared.

"I don't need therapy," Chelsea insisted. "I'm fine."

"Therapists mess you up," Nick said.

"That's not true." Demetrius helped himself to some more lemon chicken. "My cousin is a therapist and he's helped a lot of people."

The phone rang, startling them.

Nick lifted it off the coffee table. "Billy O'Reilly's," he said into the phone.

The speakerphone feature was on, so they could all hear the caller at the other end.

"Is this a bar?" an aghast voice asked.

"No, it's Billy O'Reilly's apartment," Nick explained. "Who is this?"

"This is Mrs. Jennings," a voice said. "My daughter left me this number."

"Speak of the devil," Nick muttered, handing Chelsea the phone. "You can take it in the bedroom if you want privacy."

Chelsea shook her head no and took the phone. "Mom?"

"Chelsea? Is that you?"

"Who else calls you mom?" Chelsea rolled her eyes.

"Where are you?"

"A friend's apartment," Chelsea said. "Are you okay?"

"No, I'm not okay," her mother replied, her voice rising. "I'm at a friend's house, too. You know my friend Jane Littleton, who plays the organ for the church choir? Well, I'm at her house. And would you like to know why?"

"I have a feeling I already know."

"All my life I tried to give you a good home, Chelsea. All the finest things I could afford to give you—"

"You have, Mom—"

"And this is how you repay me." Her mother's reproachful voice was trembling.

"I didn't do anything, Mom," Chelsea protested.

"You didn't?" her mother asked, a note of hysteria creeping into her voice. "Then why is our telephone at home ringing off the hook? Why is our home surrounded by reporters? They keep calling me Mrs. Kettering. That is not my name!"

"It used to be your name, Mom," Chelsea said, closing her eyes.

"It is *not* my name!" her mother repeated. "Do you see what you've done? You have ruined our lives!"

"Mom, I didn't tell!" Chelsea protested again, tears in her eyes. "Somehow they just found out—"

"I did everything so they would never find out," Chelsea's mother said, her voice shaking. "And just to get some cheap publicity, you . . . I didn't raise you to be this kind of person, Chelsea!"

"Mom, please listen!" Chelsea cried. "I didn't tell anyone. They just—"

"I have to go," her mother said, a sob in her voice. "I don't know what to do now, Chelsea."

"Mom, I—"

"The school is putting me on administrative leave," her mother went on. Karma knew that Chelsea's mother taught music at an exclusive, private school in Nashville. "The press won't leave me alone there."

"But eventually all of this will—"

"All of this will what?" her mother asked

34

tiredly. "My life is ruined, do you understand that? Did you think of me at all?"

"Mom, I'm so sorry, I—"

The phone was dead in her hand.

Wordlessly, Nick came to her and put his arms around her.

"She thinks I told," Chelsea said numbly.

"It's okay, Chels," Karma soothed. "She'll find out the truth."

"She hates me now," Chelsea said. "My own mother hates me."

"No—" Karma began.

"This is her worst nightmare come true." Tears were running down Chelsea's cheeks.

"But it's not your fault," Demetrius told her.

"Maybe it is," Chelsea insisted, wiping at her cheeks with the back of her hand. "I'm the one who went to Bigfoot to tell her the truth. I'm the one who didn't want to live my life as a lie anymore. But I never thought about what it would do to my mother."

"Chels," Nick said gently, "you can't live your life for her."

"Oh, God," Chelsea sobbed, her eyes beseeching Karma's. "What have I done? What have I done?"

But Karma didn't have any answers. All she could do was to join Nick in wrapping her arms around her friend, and letting her cry.

K arma wearily pressed her nose against the window of the Red & Tan Lines commuter bus and stared out at the suburban New Jersey landscape as the bus rumbled along the highway.

It was the next day, Friday, after work, but instead of going back to the apartment after she left the *Trash* offices, Karma had gotten on the uptown "A" subway train, taken it up to the George Washington Bridge Bus Terminal stop at 175th Street, followed the thousand of commuters streaming toward the buses that would take them home to the New Jersey and Rockland County, New York, suburbs, and boarded a bus that would take her—she hoped—to Teaneck.

Teaneck, New Jersey.

Like I ever thought I'd find myself schlepping

out to Teaneck, New Jersey, she thought ruefully. *You just never know.*

But then, I never knew I had an identical twin sister, either.

"Janelle Cho," Karma said out loud, her face still pressed against the glass. "Janelle Cho is my sister."

As the bus moved west along crowded Route 4, through Englewood and the eastern part of Teaneck, Karma marveled again as she remembered the events early in the summer that had led her, finally, to a face-to-face meeting with a girl who looked exactly like she did.

Of course, Karma knew she had been adopted as an infant. But what she hadn't known was that she apparently had an identical twin sister who had also been adopted.

And that twin sister had grown up on Staten Island.

Demetrius had insisted that he had seen Karma on the street, and she had doubted him. Karma had just felt insulted that he could actually mistake another girl for her.

I thought it was the Asian thing, she recalled. *That he thought all Asian-American girls looked alike, or something.*

But I was wrong. It was Janelle.

She looks just like me, Karma remembered. *She's spending the summer in New York, taking early classes at Columbia University. She told me she grew up on Staten Island. But I did some digging, and found out that her parents moved to Teaneck when she was in junior high school.*

I was so excited when I finally, actually met her. As Karma thought back to that day a small smile came to her lips. *To find a sister. A real, blood sister . . .*

But as things turned out, Janelle didn't want to have anything to do with Karma. She said she liked her life just fine the way it was, and she didn't want Karma in it, so would Karma just please forget she ever met her, and leave her alone?

Karma could not leave Janelle alone. Sometimes she wanted to, but she couldn't. Because Karma had been raised an only, adopted child by Marty and Wendy Kushner out on Long Island. As a Jewish girl.

And while Karma loved her parents, and was incredibly proud to be Jewish, the idea that she had a biological sister, from the same biological mother and father as she'd had, from eighteen years ago someplace in Korea, was a concept too momentous for her to ignore.

So she had called—couldn't stop herself from calling—Janelle numerous times since that fateful meeting. Janelle never wanted to talk to her for very long. Then, after a while, she simply wouldn't talk to Karma. She just refused to take Karma's calls, and ignored the messages Karma would leave on her answering machine.

And now there was simply no answer at Janelle's dorm room.

She must be on some kind of break from classes, Karma thought as the bus passed a long line of gas stations on the right-hand side of the road. *Which means she's probably home with her parents, in Teaneck.*

I must be out of my mind to go out to her parents' house, unannounced, to see her. I didn't even tell anyone I was going. Not Chelsea, or Lisha, or Demetrius.

Because they all would have told me not to come, Karma realized. *They would have said I need to respect Janelle's wishes. And that all that will happen is that I'll get my heart broken in person instead of over the phone.*

But I have to see her. I just have to.

The bus passed Teaneck High School on the left, and then Queen Anne Road and Belle Avenue, before pulling off Route 4 at the Fairleigh Dickinson University exit and River Road.

"You'll tell me when we get to West Englewood Avenue?" Karma asked the bus driver. Since she'd never been to Teaneck before, she'd deliberately sat up front, near the driver. "I'm kind of lost here."

"You got it," the middle-aged African-American driver said to her. "It's just up here about a mile or so on the right." He made a sharp left turn onto River Road.

And then, a few minutes later, he was stopping at a traffic light.

"West Englewood Avenue," he said to Karma. "Your stop, miss."

"Thanks," Karma said as the driver opened the automatic door for her. She stepped down the two steps off the bus and watched as it pulled away, in a cloud of noxious black diesel smoke, leaving her alone in a suburban landscape that looked a lot like where she'd grown up on Long Island.

"Okay, I'm here," Karma announced, to no one in particular, scanning her surroundings. Across the street was a park, with swings and a merry-go-round. Two little girls were playing with their father.

That's how Janelle and I might have played, she thought, *if we had stayed together as—*

Karma cut off this line of thought.

It was too painful.

She looked down at the sheet of paper she'd taken out of her pocket and carefully unfolded it: *808 West Englewood Avenue,* it read. *Henry and Muriel Cho.*

There was only one way to go, as West Englewood Avenue dead-ended into River Road. Karma turned right and started to walk up the gently sloping hill that was West Englewood Avenue.

She didn't need to walk far. The Cho house was the third one on the right-hand side.

It was as unassuming as it could be—a medium-size frame house with a smallish front lawn. A tan Honda Accord was parked in the driveway.

"I must be out of my mind," Karma mumbled

41

as she walked up the driveway toward the front door.

She rang the bell.

The door opened. There stood a petite, attractive, Korean-looking woman, in her mid-forties.

"Janelle!" she exclaimed. "Did you forget your keys again? And you went shopping! Look at those clothes!"

Karma had on the outfit she'd worn to work that day—hot-pink flared pants with suspenders over a cropped polyester shirt in a wild, colorful print that bared her stomach. Her hair was up in a high, long-ponytail with a row of tiny flower barrettes in various colors.

"Is it some kind of costume, Janelle?" the woman asked her uncertainly.

Karma knew that Janelle dressed in the most ordinary, preppiest of clothes, kind of like Chelsea.

Janelle would never, ever, ever wear this outfit, she realized.

"I'm not Janelle," Karma said softly.

The woman just stared at her.

"My name is Karma Kushner. I think I'm Janelle's twin sister."

The woman kept staring at her. She didn't blink.

And then, she slumped to the floor in a dead faint.

•   •   •

"Janelle didn't say anything about you," Muriel Cho said softly. She was a small woman, five-two or so, with soft, dark hair that fell to her shoulders. She was dressed as if she'd just stepped off the golf course, in khaki shorts and a white golf shirt.

"Not a word," her husband, Henry, added. He shook his head and stared at Karma. "My God. You look just like her." His hair was short, and he was as ordinary looking as his wife. He, too, looked like he was dressed for golf.

"I do look just like her," Karma said. "I mean, it shocked me, too, when we met."

It was ten minutes later. Henry had come into the hallway just as his wife fainted. He took one look at Karma and went slack-jawed. Then he regained his composure enough to pull some smelling salts out of a first-aid box in the front hall closet and give them to his wife. She regained consciousness immediately.

And then the two Chos invited Karma into their living room. Janelle was out, they said. She wasn't getting back until late. In the meantime could Karma please explain to them who she was, and where she came from, and what she knew about their daughter, Janelle?

Karma did just that, quickly.

"I can't believe it." Muriel touched her hand to her cheek in disbelief. "I'm sitting here looking at you and . . . I still can't believe it."

"Not a word. Not a word." Henry marveled,

repeating himself again and again. "Janelle didn't say a word about ever meeting you."

Karma tried not to let that knowledge hurt her, but it did.

So that's how much it meant to her that she met me, that I even exist, she thought. *She didn't even tell her parents.*

"When we adopted Janelle," Mrs. Cho began, "we never knew there was . . . I mean, we were told that she was an only child."

"That's what my parents were told, too," Karma said. She took a sip of water from the glass they had given her.

"You told them about Janelle?" Mr. Cho asked.

"Yeah," Karma said. "I've been pretty freaked out about this, you know?"

"I can imagine." Mrs. Cho clucked sympathetically. "So, have you and our daughter become friends?"

Karma shook her head no. "Frankly, she hasn't been very interested in getting to know me," she confessed. "She told me she's happy with her life and basically she didn't want me disrupting it."

"I see," Mr. Cho said, nodding.

"But I don't *want* to disrupt it," Karma said quickly. "I mean, I don't expect her to, like, become my best friend. Unless, of course, she wants to."

Janelle's parents just stared at her implacably as she talked.

"So!" Karma exclaimed, her voice a shade too bright. "Tell me about you."

"Not much to tell," Henry said. "I'm head of guidance at Thomas Jefferson Middle School here in Teaneck, my wife teaches mathematics at the high school. Janelle is our only daughter. As you know, we adopted her."

"And we love her very much," Mrs. Cho added.

"What's she like?" Karma asked.

"You mean the two of you haven't gotten to know each other?" Mrs. Cho was clearly surprised.

"Well, like I said," Karma explained, "she didn't want to get real buddy-buddy with me. But I really think that if she got to know me, she'd like me, you know? Hey, I look just like her! How different can we be, right?"

"Well, we'd be glad to tell you something about Janelle," Mr. Cho said. "For one thing, she is a wonderful student."

"Very hardworking," Mrs. Cho added proudly. "Straight A's. Did you get straight A's, too?"

"Not hardly," Karma admitted.

"And she certainly doesn't dress anything like you do," Mrs. Cho observed, taking in Karma's outfit again. "You have . . . courageous taste."

Karma laughed. "I'll take that as a compliment. What else? What's she studying?"

"Economics," Mr. Cho replied. "She wants to get her undergraduate degree in economics, and then get an MBA and work for a big Wall Street investment firm."

"Stock market analyst, maybe," Mrs. Cho added.

"No kidding?" Karma marveled. "Too cool!"

"Why is that?" Mr. Cho asked politely.

"Stock market analyst!" Karma said. "It makes perfect sense!" She got so excited that some of the water in her glass spilled over onto her lap. "I invest in the market, I made a lot of money in the market—I *love* the market! Wow, it must be some genetic thing, huh?"

"Perhaps it is," Mrs. Cho murmured.

"So, what else?" Karma asked eagerly.

"Let's see," Mrs. Cho mused, "she doesn't sleep much. She has more energy than anyone else I've ever known. And she loves to eat junk food."

"Double bingo!" Karma cried. "Triple, even!"

Muriel and Henry looked at each other.

"Can I see her room?" Karma asked hopefully. "I mean, I don't mean to pry, but—"

"I don't see why not," Mrs. Cho answered, getting to her feet. She led Karma out of the living room and up a flight of stairs. She opened one of the doors at the top of the stairs, and Karma stepped into Janelle's bedroom.

"Barbies," Karma whispered, looking at a shelf loaded with dolls.

"You love Barbies?" Muriel asked.

"Hated Barbie," Karma said. "But I collected Ken dolls when I was a kid. I used to put makeup on Ken and make girls' clothes for him."

"You what?" Mrs. Cho looked somewhat confused.

"Oh, well, it was much more of a challenge to make Ken look cute than to make Barbie look cute," Karma explained.

Muriel smiled. "I see."

Henry Cho climbed the stairs to join his wife and Karma outside Janelle's room.

"Karma—" he began.

"Hey, does Janelle happen to have an entire collection of cashmere sweaters?" she asked eagerly. "Because that would be really eerie. I have, like, a zillion of them, and—"

"Karma," Mr. Cho said again. "I don't want to be rude. And it was nice of you to go through the trouble of coming out here. But . . . we are going to have to ask you to leave."

Karma looked bewildered. "Was it something I did? I didn't mean to ask about her clothes. I mean, if that's too personal—"

"It isn't the clothes," Mr. Cho said. "Please, let's go downstairs."

They returned to the living room.

"Our daughter is not a child anymore," Mr. Cho explained. "She's eighteen. She's beginning college. We must respect her wishes. And apparently her wish is that her life be separate from yours."

"But . . . but . . . you were both so nice to me before," Karma stammered.

47

"You are a guest in our home," Mr. Cho said.

Karma looked over at Mrs. Cho, who was looking at her husband with a face neither approving nor disapproving. It was simply impassive.

What's that face supposed to mean? Karma thought. *My mother has never looked that way at my father in her entire life.*

"Will you tell Janelle I came here?" she asked them meekly.

"No," Henry said. "I'm sorry."

"But—"

"I was thinking just now, while you and my wife were looking at Janelle's room," Mr. Cho said. "And I felt very troubled about this. We have to respect Janelle's privacy. If Janelle felt otherwise, everything would be different. But for now, no."

"So you mean to tell me that just like she kept it a secret from you that she ever met me, you're going to keep it a secret from her that you ever met me."

"That's right." Mr. Cho nodded.

"Gee," Karma said, "it's kind of like I don't even exist." She had meant it to come out as a joke, but she felt a hard, sad lump form in her throat.

Pulling herself together, she stood up. "It was nice meeting you," she managed.

"You, too, Karma," Mrs. Cho said softly, reaching out for Karma's hand.

"I hope Janelle . . . oh, it doesn't matter,"

Karma said, fighting to keep herself from crying.

She fought it all the way to the front door, and continued to do so as she stepped outside.

But when she was waiting for the Red & Tan Lines bus that would take her back to New York City, she noticed, standing on the other side of River Road, the two sisters she'd seen earlier. They were still playing with their daddy in the park. Their laughter and giggles carried easily in the summer evening air.

And that's when the tears came for Karma.

And for a sister who didn't seem to care if she was dead or alive.

4

*O*kay, so what if you have a twin sister who hates your guts, Karma told herself as she let herself into the apartment that evening. She juggled her keys with the bag of groceries she'd stopped to buy. *It's her loss.*

"I hate that telephone!" Chelsea was yelling as Karma walked in.

"And it's not fond of you, either," Karma joked, taking her groceries into the kitchen. "What's up?"

"The whole world is after me," Chelsea said, staring daggers at the phone. "Every talk show wants me to come on and talk about my life. Every newspaper and magazine wants an interview."

Karma came into the living room and sat in the overstuffed chair. "So why don't you just unplug the phone again?"

"I've been letting the answering machine pick

up," Chelsea explained. "It really isn't fair to you and Lisha for us to not have a working phone."

"And I plead guilty of being the one to point it out to her," Lisha said, entering the living room from the hall. "Besides, she has to deal with the vultures sooner or later."

"At least the press isn't standing in front of the apartment building anymore," Karma noted.

"Big deal," Chelsea snorted. "Look at this!" She waved a small pad of paper at Karma. "This is full of phone messages for Chelsea Kettering, daughter of psycho shooter Charles Kettering. It's disgusting."

"Never underestimate the public's interest in the macabre," Lisha said.

"How trashy it is," Karma added, using Jazz's new pet phrase.

Lisha went into the kitchen and stuck her head in the bag of groceries Karma had bought. "Chocolate-chip cookies, Doritos, potato chips, dip . . . Karma, this is all junk food!"

"I know," Karma said. "I had a bad day. I need comfort."

"Me, too," Lisha decided, breaking open the bag of chips. "So, what happened?"

"I went to see my so-called sister," Karma said, "and . . . never mind."

"Why?" Lisha asked, returning to the living room. "What happened?"

"I don't want to talk about it," Karma said. "It's too stupid and depressing."

"Listen, Karma," Lisha began, "it's her loss if she doesn't appreciate how great you are, and—"

The phone rang.

"Go away and leave me alone!" Chelsea yelled at it, putting her hands over her ears.

Karma reached over and snatched it up. "Hello?"

"This is Margie Pearson," a perky voice said. "Is this Chelsea Kettering?"

"No," Karma said bluntly.

"I'm a producer with *Fast Copy*," the woman said smoothly. "You know, the newsmagazine show."

"You mean the creepy, icky, scandal-sheet show," Karma corrected, beginning to enjoy herself.

"We happen to be a very ethical show," the producer told her defensively. "We recently exposed a crack mother who was neglecting her five children, which resulted in—"

"Can we cut to the chase here?" Karma interrupted. "What did you want?"

"I'd like to speak to Chelsea Kettering, if she's there," Margie said.

"Why?" Karma demanded.

"To invite her on our show," the producer said. "We would treat her like a queen, and—"

"Chels, you want to be on *Fast Copy*?" Karma yelled across the room.

"God, no," Chelsea said, making a face.

"She isn't interested," Karma told the producer.

"But—"

"Sorry," Karma said. "Have a wonderful life and don't call back." She hung up the phone. "That was very satisfying," she announced, then got up and reached into the bag of chips that Lisha was eating.

"I wish you'd just handle all the calls," Chelsea moaned. "The only person I want to talk to is my mother, and she isn't speaking to me anymore."

"She'll get over it," Lisha mumbled, her mouth full of chips.

"I don't know if she will," Chelsea said. "All these years she's kept it this big secret, and now—"

"And now she has to face the truth," Lisha finished, shrugging.

"It's not so simple," Chelsea insisted. "She told me she got suspended from her job. What if they don't take her back?"

"They can't fire her over this," Karma said.

"How do you know?" Chelsea asked.

"I don't," Karma admitted. "But it sounds to me like it's a violation of some right, or something. Ask a lawyer."

"I can't afford to ask a lawyer," Chelsea said.

"You can if you go on one of these sleazy shows," Lisha said, reaching her hand into the chips bag again. "I bet they'd pay you big bucks."

"Nah." Karma shook her head. "They try to induce you to come on their show, saying that they are the only ones who will tell the true story of Chelsea Kettering."

"In other words, they're cheap," Lisha translated.

"How do you know?" Chelsea asked.

Karma went to the kitchen counter and pulled the chocolate-chip cookies out of the grocery bag. "I have this older cousin, Ernie Kushner—a total sleaze-bucket kind of guy who doesn't deserve the name Kushner, by the by—who interned a few summers ago on *Jenny Jones*. I got the dish."

"So what happened to him?" Lisha asked.

"He went into politics," Karma said, chomping on a cookie.

Chelsea buried her head under a pillow she grabbed from the couch.

"My own mother told me I ruined her life," she moaned.

"I'm telling you, Chels, she'll get over it," Lisha insisted. "And just think about how well Nick took it."

"That's true." Chelsea took the pillow off her face, and a secretive smile lifted the corners of her mouth. "He's been so great."

The phone rang again. Karma snatched it up. "Hello?"

Chelsea screamed and covered her face with the pillow again.

"Hi, there," a smooth, male voice said in Karma's ear. "This is David Yancy, from the *Geraldo* show."

"Uh-huh," Karma said, trying her best to sound utterly bored.

"Might I speak with Chelsea Jennings?"

"At least you got her name right," Karma said. "Two points for you."

"Thank you," David responded. "Is she in?"

"She's in, but she can't come to the phone."

"I see," David said. "And to whom am I speaking?"

"This is her agent," Karma ad-libbed. "My name is Kushner. Karma Kushner."

"My *agent*?" Chelsea echoed.

Karma covered the receiver. "I make it up as I go along," she said with a shrug, then put her ear back to the phone.

"What agency are you with?" Yancy asked Karma.

"The Kushner Agency," Karma said, doing her best imitation of an irritated executive. "You have a problem with that?"

"I've never heard of your agency," Yancy replied superciliously.

"Well, now you have," Karma said sweetly. And then she hung up on him.

"Wow, this is so much fun!" she told her friends, and reached into the bag for another cookie. "My mood is rapidly improving."

The phone rang again.

"Kushner Agency," Karma barked into the phone.

Lisha and Chelsea both stifled laughs, Chelsea more successfully than Lisha, who actually spewed a couple of small potato chip bits onto the floor. This made Chelsea crack up even more.

"Yancy here. Sorry that I disconnected you just now."

Karma put her hand over the receiver and laughed. "You guys!" she told her friend gleefully. "This is too hilarious! I hung up on this guy and he's, like, falling all over himself to take responsibility for it!"

"This could be a whole new career for you," Lisha said.

Karma uncovered the phone. "So, Yancy— what show are you with again—*60 Minutes*?"

"Has *60 Minutes* already called?" Yancy asked, panicked. "I'm with *Geraldo.*"

"Yeah," Karma said. "Right. Look, Yance, babe, I haven't got all night. Time is money. What do you want?"

"We want Chelsea on *Geraldo.*"

"What for?"

"We want to do a feature on her."

"So does everyone else in the media world," Karma snapped. "What are you going to do differently?"

There was a moment's silence, before Yancy could formulate a reply. Clearly, he hadn't given much thought to anything beyond simply getting Chelsea to appear on Geraldo's famous talk show.

"We'll . . . give her the entire hour," Yancy said.

"Yeah?" Karma asked. "And what else?"

"What else would you want?" Yancy asked.

"Hey, you called me," Karma reminded him. "How about you think about it some more, and call me back tomorrow."

"But—"

"Not tonight," Karma said firmly. "Tomorrow. Do you understand?"

"Tomorrow," Yancy repeated, his voice meek.

"Good," Karma said. "You're getting the idea." She hung up the phone. "You know, Lish, you're right." She reached for another cookie as she went on. "I really am beginning to think about revising my career choice. I've got this down, huh?"

"You sound like a middle-aged guy with a cigar clamped between his teeth, wheeling and dealing," Lisha said, laughing.

"Yeah, it's a genes thing," Karma whined.

"You're fantastic!" Chelsea told her. "Really. And I can't tell you what a relief it is to have you answering the phone."

"I sort of like the idea of the William Morris–Kushner Agency," Karma mused, fusing her name with that of one of the most famous talent agencies of all time. "It has a certain ring to it, don't you think?"

The phone rang again. This time, Lisha went to get it, gulping down one last mouthful of potato chips en route.

"Kushner Agency," she breathed, in her sexiest, smokiest voice. "May I help you? . . . Yes, we handle Miss Jennings. One moment for Miss Kushner, please." She thrust the phone at Karma, laughing again.

"Kushner," Karma barked into the phone.

"Miss Kushner, this is Lewis Ricorda," an imperious haughty male voice intoned.

There was an expectant pause, as if the man expected Karma to know who he was and be suitably impressed.

Karma had no idea who he was. And while a lesser agent, trying to impress a client or make a prospective deal, might have acted with Ricorda as if she did indeed know who he was, and was suitably impressed, Karma would have none of that.

She just held the phone to her ear and waited.

"Don't you know who I am?" the man finally asked.

"Not really," Karma said. "Why don't you tell me?"

"Have you ever heard of Sunnybrook Books?" Ricorda asked.

Karma had heard of Sunnybrook. They were one of the larger publishing houses in New York. There had been a feature about them in a recent *Business Week* magazine that she'd read. They'd just acquired the autobiography of a famous, ten-year-old child movie star for a half-million dollars, and the industry was buzzing about it.

"Of course I know Sunnybrook, Ricorda," Karma said, deliberately calling the man by his last name. "And yeah, you're the V.P. and publisher. Now, could you tell me why you're calling my client on a Friday night?"

"I have something very important I want to discuss with her," Ricorda said.

"Discuss it with me," Karma said. "I'm her agent, remember?" She began to pace with the phone, warming to the role.

"Okay," Ricorda agreed. "Sunnybrook is interested in acquiring the worldwide rights to Chelsea's autobiography."

Karma laughed. And then she laughed some more.

"What's so funny?" Ricorda asked.

"Do you know, Lew—may I call you Lew?—do you know, Lew, how many publishers have already called who want the rights to Chelsea's autobiography?"

"No other publishers have—" Chelsea began, but Karma quickly shushed her.

"Perhaps many have called," Ricorda said, "but they are not Sunnybrook. We want Miss Jennings to have the chance to tell her own story, and—"

Karma yawned ostentatiously into the phone. "What time is it, Lew?"

"It's . . . uh, ten-fifteen," he replied.

"Uh-huh," Karma said. "My client needs her beauty sleep. And so do I. So can the chitchat. Let's talk money."

"We're willing to offer a large advance," Ricorda said to Karma.

"How large?" Karma asked, knowing that an

advance was the amount that a book publisher paid to an author before the author's manuscript was actually completed.

"A half-million dollars," Ricorda said. "And I'll edit it myself."

"A half million," Karma repeated for Chelsea and Lisha's benefit. Chelsea's jaw fell open with shock.

"Don't yank my chain, Lew," Karma snapped into the phone. "That's what you paid the kid!" She was thoroughly enjoying this.

"Well, yes, but—"

"That kid is ten years old! He hasn't done anything. He's not Chelsea Kettering!"

"Okay," Ricorda said hastily. "You've got a point. A million."

"A million seven-fifty," Karma countered, whimsically suggesting that Sunnybrook pay Chelsea $1,750,000 for the right to publish the story of her life.

"A million-five, take it or leave it," Ricorda said.

"Call me Monday," Karma said. "I need to talk to my client."

She hung up the telephone.

Chelsea's face was the color of typing paper. "A million seven-fifty? For *what*?"

"It's just a million-five," Karma said nonchalantly. "Sorry, I tried to get you more. It was a tough negotiation."

"Holy sugar on a shingle," Lisha breathed. "They want to pay you one million five hundred thousand dollars for your story, Chelsea! You'll be set for life!"

"This can't really be happening," Chelsea said faintly. "I must be dreaming."

"It's happening," Lisha assured her. "Karma, you're a genius!"

"True," Karma said immodestly.

"But why?" Chelsea asked. "Why would a publisher want to—"

"I don't think you realize how big this is," Lisha said. "America is fascinated with this sick stuff."

"A million and a half," Karma mused. "Let's see, as your agent I get ten percent, which gives me a cool hundred and fifty thousand. This is even better than the stock market!"

Chelsea just shook her head. "Y'all, I can't even . . . I can't even grasp this."

"Grasp what, that you're about to become fabulously wealthy?" Lisha asked.

"If she accepts Lew's offer, that is," Karma added. She cocked her head at Chelsea. "You *are* going to do it, aren't you? Chels?"

But Chelsea didn't answer. She just sat there.

"Chelsea?" Lisha asked. "You're not really going to turn down a million and a half dollars.

"Are you?"

5

Karma and Chelsea walked east on West Seventy-second Street, heading for the bagel factory on Broadway, which, they had determined through a rigorous process of elimination, baked the very best bagels in the western hemisphere. The Saturday-morning sunshine was so bright as to almost be blinding—it promised to be another one of those hot, humid July days for which New York City is justly famous.

It was the next morning, around eleven o'clock. The girls—and the guys, since they'd dropped in around midnight—had stayed up talking until nearly two o'clock, about the events of the past week, and about the Sunnybrook Books offer for Chelsea to write her autobiography for $1.5 million.

Now, though, Chelsea and Karma were on a

mission to buy fresh bagels and cream cheese for breakfast.

"You know you gotta take the cash," Karma told Chelsea for the zillionth time.

"I don't know anything," Chelsea replied as she and Karma moved to the left on the sidewalk in order to avoid a couple of female joggers who were running toward Riverside Drive.

"But it's a fortune!" Karma exclaimed. "You can't turn down a fortune!"

"It just . . . I don't know. It doesn't seem right."

"It'll seem a lot less objectionable when you're really, really rich," Karma assured her.

"But what about the ethics of it?" Chelsea wondered.

"What?" Karma questioned. "It's not like you did anything wrong."

"I know that," Chelsea said. "But if my father hadn't done . . . what he did, no one would be giving me the time of day."

"That's true," Karma agreed. They walked farther down the block. "Isn't it amazing that no reporters are trailing us?"

"We live in a disposable world," Chelsea said.

"Yeah, on to the next victim," Karma agreed. "How trashy it is!"

Chelsea nodded. "I don't really want to add to the trash in the world, if you know what I mean."

"But it's not like you'd be going on a talk

show and spilling your guts," Karma pointed out. "You'd be writing a book."

"True," Chelsea allowed. "I guess writing a book is different—"

"You said 'ratting a book,'" Karma noted.

"No," Chelsea said. She moved to sidestep what looked to be a professional dog walker who was trying to pass them, with six or seven various-sized canines in tow. "I said 'writing.'"

"You said 'ratting,'" Karma repeated.

"My Tennessee accent, I guess—"

"No," Karma said. "It's more like you think writing a book would be ratting out your mother."

Chelsea stopped and looked at her. "You're kidding."

"I'm serious. I should be a shrink. A shrink *and* an agent!"

"Well, maybe I *would* be hurting my mom," Chelsea said as they started walking again. "It's not like I can ask her her opinion. She isn't speaking to me." They turned left onto Broadway.

"The thing is," she mused, "if I did it, I could never keep the money."

"Are you crazy?" Karma asked. "Who would you give it to?"

"The families of the people my dad killed," Chelsea said thoughtfully.

"But I thought you told me that there were like a whole bunch of lawsuits after the shootings," Karma reminded her. "And that your dad's estate had to pay out like a gazillion dollars to the families."

That was true. Charles Kettering had been a successful lawyer who'd invested his assets carefully. At the time of his death he'd amassed a considerable fortune. All of which had been paid out to his victims' families, leaving Chelsea and her mom with precious little money.

"We did," Chelsea admitted.

"Then I'd say that debt was paid for," Karma stated firmly. "*You* didn't shoot them. Your dad did. Don't you think you and your mom have suffered enough?"

"Karma, that debt could never be paid!" Chelsea replied.

The two of them turned into the bagel factory, which had the not-so-lofty name Broadway Hot Bagels.

"A dozen and a half garlic and sesame seed bagels," Karma told the Semitic-looking guy at the cash register. "And a pound of chives cream cheese."

"Yeah, sure," the guy said to her, and then yelled something in Arabic to his coworkers behind him.

"Hey," Karma said to the guy, "I never asked you. What country are you guys from?"

"Egypt," the counterman said, with a big smile.

"You gotta love New York," Karma said, turning to Chelsea. "Immigrant guys from Egypt, who are probably Muslim, open a bagel factory in New York City and sell Jewish food to New Yorkers. Only in New York."

In a few moments the girls' order had been assembled and bagged. They waited for the counterman to ring up the sale on the register.

"You know," Karma said, "if you take the book deal, you're going to get famous all over again, when the book pubs."

"I know," Chelsea said ruefully. "I hate that part of it."

"You're so bizarre, Chels." Karma shook her head. "Most girls would kill for fame and wealth—no pun intended—and you're freaked out by it."

"Don't you see, Karma?" Chelsea asked. "I didn't do anything to earn it. I can't . . . I don't know, sing or dance. I didn't cure cancer. This is all happening because of a terrible tragedy. It just feels so wrong to me."

Karma put her hand on Chelsea's. "I understand."

"Do you?"

"Yeah," Karma told her. "Really. I do."

Chelsea sighed. "My mom really could use the money, though."

"I thought you just told me that you couldn't keep the money if you did it," Karma reminded her.

"Well, my mom isn't me." She sighed again. "I am so confused."

Just then, a guy in his mid-twenties, dressed

in black jeans and a Tim McGraw T-shirt, approached Chelsea and Karma.

"You're Chelsea Jennings," the guy said to Chelsea with a thick Southern accent. "Aren't you?"

Chelsea nodded. "That's right," she said wearily, her hopes of getting through the day as just another ordinary girl in New York City immediately shattered.

"I'm Billy Slocum," the guy said. "I'm real happy to meet you."

"I'm happy to meet you, too," Chelsea returned politely, like the well-bred Southern girl she was. "This is my friend Karma Kushner."

"Agent," Karma corrected. "Kushner Agency. I handle Chelsea."

"You're nothing like what I thought you'd be like," Billy told Chelsea.

Chelsea stood there uncomfortably, and looked over at the counterman. He was chatting with his coworkers, in no hurry to ring up their bagels.

"Well, nice to meet you, Billy," she said, moving toward the counter.

"Just a sec." Billy stepped forward to stop her. "I really wanted to talk to you."

"Listen, Billy," Karma interjected, "she would really appreciate it if people would just kind of leave her alone now, okay?"

Billy nodded. "I guess I thought my name would sound familiar to her."

Chelsea overheard the question. "No," she said, "I have no idea who you are."

"Billy Slocum," he repeated. "Slow-come. It should sound familiar to you. Think about it."

Karma looked at Chelsea, who had a puzzled look on her face.

Then Karma saw her expression turn to shock.

Chelsea walked back over to Billy. "Is . . . is your father—was your father Earl Slocum?"

The boy nodded. He pulled out his wallet, took a photo out of it, and thrust it at Chelsea.

Chelsea took it, looked at the photo quickly, and handed it to Karma.

It was obviously the same guy, except he was seven or eight years old. He was posed with a couple of younger kids and a man who looked like a slightly older version of the guy himself, and a woman who had to be the man's wife.

They were in front of a building with a sign on it that read JOHNSON CITY COURTHOUSE.

"This was the last picture that was taken of my whole family," Billy said, his voice now cracking with emotion. "The last picture before . . . you know."

Karma's hand—the one holding the photo— began to shake. Because she had just put two and two together.

Billy Slocum's dad, Earl Slocum, is one of the people who was killed in the Burger Barn shooting by Chelsea's father, she realized.

This is Chelsea's worst nightmare come true.

"I'm so sorry," Chelsea began, her voice low. "If there's anything I can do—"

"That's not why I'm here," Billy interrupted. "I came to thank you."

To thank her? Karma thought. *But why?*

"What . . . why should you thank me?" Chelsea asked, tears in her eyes and a desperate note in her voice. "I thought you would hate me."

"I don't," Billy said. "I mean, I reckon it's real hard to live with knowing what your daddy did."

"It is," Chelsea confirmed simply.

By now, the Egyptian counterman had returned to the cash register and was waiting patiently for the girls to pay for their bagels, but they didn't notice.

"Why do you want to thank her?" Karma asked.

"For how she is," Billy said earnestly. He turned to Chelsea. "For how you're doing all this."

"Doing what?" Chelsea asked.

"I seen what happened on *Trash*," Billy went on. "I guess the whole world is after you now, huh? All those talk shows and stuff? But I don't see you going on any of them. And I bet they're all throwing a heap of money at you, too."

"A little," Chelsea admitted.

"Well, you're doing good now. So don't you take it," Billy said fervently. "Don't you take a dime of it."

"I—"

"Don't you take it, Chelsea," Billy repeated, his jaw trembling. "That's blood money."

Chelsea stood there, mute.

"Blood money," he repeated. "You hear me? Well, that's all I got to say." He turned, and left the bakery.

But his words rang in Karma's ears.

Don't you take it, Chelsea. Blood money. You hear me?

"You're gonna love this place," Karma told Demetrius as he swung open the door to a new downtown dance club called Poodles.

It was that evening, and although Karma usually had to work at Jimi's, the hot downtown club where she worked on Saturday nights, this week the owner had given her both last night and tonight off. So, of course, she was spending it with Demetrius.

Karma had read about Poodles in the *Voice* the week before, and she'd been dying to go there ever since. Like Jimi's, this club did not serve alcohol. It had a fifties theme. All the waitresses wore poodle skirts and saddle shoes. The dance music was all old rock and roll. They regularly held contests for look-alikes of John Travolta and Olivia Newton-John from the old movie *Grease*.

Karma had dressed for the occasion. She wore a poodle skirt shortened to micro-mini length, with an extra-small man's white T-

71

shirt, white fishnet hose, and white go-go boots. Demetrius had refused to dress any way except the way he always dressed, in jeans and a black T-shirt.

The music hit them as soon as they entered the club, something upbeat by Jerry Lee Lewis.

"Ten-dollar cover," the bored girl at the door told them. She was a gorgeous blonde, wearing a fifties outfit featuring a tight, red sweater and a long, straight, black skirt.

Demetrius handed her ten dollars.

"That's ten dollars each," the girl said, still holding her hand out. She grinned at Demetrius. "Of course, if it were up to me, you could come in for free."

Demetrius handed her ten more dollars.

"Have a blast from the past," the girl told Demetrius, completely ignoring Karma. "By the way, my name is Colleen, in case you need me for anything."

"Thank you, Miss Welcome Wagon," Karma droned as she and Demetrius walked to one of the few empty booths that surrounded the crowded, oversized dance floor.

"That's a high cover charge for a place with recorded music," Demetrius commented, sliding into the booth next to Karma.

"I read that sometimes they have special guest artists show up and perform," Karma told him. "Like, last week, Tori Amos showed up."

"She doesn't do fifties music," Demetrius said.

"Would you turn down a chance to have Tori Amos sing if it was your club?" Karma asked.

"Good point."

"Hi," a waitress said, coming over to the table. She was, if possible, even cuter than Colleen. "What can I get for you?"

"A Coke," Karma said.

"The same," Demetrius added.

"There's a ten-dollar-per-person minimum at the table," the waitress pointed out. "Here you order food. If you just want Cokes, you should go to the bar."

Demetrius sighed. "Where's the menu?"

"There isn't one," the waitress said. "We have burgers, dogs, fries, and onion rings."

"So how are we supposed to order ten dollars' worth of food?" Demetrius asked.

"The burgers are ten," the waitress was kind enough to inform him.

Demetrius shook his head with disgust.

"Bring us two burgers and two fries," Karma ordered. The waitress walked away.

"I really hate getting ripped off like this," Demetrius said over the music.

"We're paying for atmosphere," Karma pointed out. "And I read that lots of famous people hang out here."

"When I have my restaurant," Demetrius said, "we'll have fair prices for great food."

Oh yeah, that's right, Karma recalled. *His*

dream is to open his own restaurant. And he's trying to save up money to get it started.

She reached for his hand. "I'm sorry. I didn't know it was so pricey here. You want me to pay half?"

"Nope," he said. He leaned over and kissed her cheek, and she leaned against him, watching the couples on the dance floor jitterbugging to the old rock and roll.

Just think, Karma mused, *Chelsea wouldn't have to worry about something like a high cover charge at a club ever again.*

Unless, of course, she actually does turn down the money.

She had told Demetrius all about the offer from Sunnybrook Books. He had been astounded. And, like Chelsea, he had not been instantly sure it was something she should do.

"But as her agent I'd make a heap of cash on this deal," Karma had pointed out to him.

"Karma, money isn't that important," had been Demetrius' reply.

"Wanna bet?" Karma had retorted.

I guess Demetrius is just more evolved than I am, she decided now as she gazed at his chiseled profile. *It's not that I think money is everything, but it sure is a lot.*

"Want to dance?" she asked Demetrius.

"I don't know how to jitterbug," he said.

"Okay, we'll wait for a slow one," Karma told him, snuggling against him again.

"Hi, there." Karma looked up to see Colleen, the girl from the door.

"Hi," Demetrius said.

"Having fun?"

"Sure," he replied.

"I'd love to dance with you later," Colleen told him, pretending that Karma didn't exist. "I get a break in a half hour."

"I'm with someone," Demetrius said pointedly.

Colleen looked over at Karma, as if seeing her for the first time. "Oh."

"Oh, yourself," Karma interjected.

Colleen looked Demetrius' diminutive date over, then looked back at Demetrius. "Did anyone ever tell you you look like that guy who models for the romance novels, what's-his-name?"

"Fabio?" Karma filled in.

"Yeah, him," Colleen said. "Only darker. So, are you two married? To each other, I mean."

"No," Karma replied.

Colleen gave Karma a cool look. "Well, then, I guess he can dance with anyone he wants to dance with," she concluded with impeccable logic.

"See you soon, I hope," she added to Demetrius, then sauntered off.

"This stuff happens to you all the time." Karma sighed, marveling.

"No, it doesn't—"

"Yeah, it does," Karma insisted. "You're like some kind of girl magnet."

"Come on, Karma—"

"I'm serious," she said. "It would take me and my identical twin to just guard your oversized body!"

"Speaking of twins, have you talked to her lately?" Demetrius asked.

"Hey, hey, we're not changing the subject so easily," Karma protested.

"Look, I have no interest in dancing with Colleen. She's an airhead. And she's rude. Okay?"

"Okay," Karma said. "But you could if you wanted to. I mean, it's a free country, I'm not possessive—"

"Karma," Demetrius said, "I don't want to."

"Okay. Cool."

"So have you talked to Janelle?"

"No," Karma said. "But I did talk to her parents. In person."

And then she told him every detail about her trip to Teaneck the day before.

"Unbelievable," Demetrius said when she had finished. "Families are so weird. They're going to pretend they never even met you, huh? Just like she pretends you don't exist."

"Evidently."

"I know that hurts your feelings," he said softly.

"Nah," Karma scoffed. She watched a guy and girl dancing who were good enough to be in some kind of competition.

76

Demetrius turned her face to him. "I know you better than that."

"Okay, maybe a little," she admitted.

"A lot," Demetrius corrected. "If one of my brothers pretended I didn't exist, I'd want to cry."

"Well, not me," Karma maintained. "It's her loss, ya know?"

"Oh, right," he said, laughing. "You're so tough."

"I *am* tough!"

The music had changed to a ballad. Demetrius slid out of the booth just as the waitress brought their food to the table. He held out his hand to Karma. "Come on and dance with me."

"But the food just got here—"

"Come on," Demetrius said, taking her hand.

They walked onto the dance floor, and Demetrius took her into his arms. He was so much larger than she was that she was enveloped in the muscular warmth of his embrace.

"I could do chin-ups on your biceps," Karma pointed out.

Demetrius laughed. "You're so romantic." He pulled her closer. Leaning down, he began to sing into her ear: "I only have eyes for you. . . ."

Then he softly kissed her neck, her cheek, right next to her mouth, as they slowly swayed to the music.

"I'll give you an hour to stop that," Karma murmured.

"I'll take it," Demetrius promised, gently gathering her hair off the back of her neck.

Okay, this is just about totally perfect, she thought as she closed her eyes and gave herself up to the moment. *I'm here in Demetrius' arms, he wants to be with me, he has no interest in Colleen, or any other girl, for that matter, except tiny me.*

Demetrius kissed her again. She stood on tiptoe to kiss him back, inhaling the delicious scent of his cologne.

The music ended, but Demetrius and Karma kept kissing.

"Get a room!" someone yelled to them.

Karma opened her eyes. She was dangling in the air, in Demetrius' arms.

"Guess we'd better sit down," Demetrius said, chagrined. He took Karma's hand and led her back to the table.

As they took their seats a balding guy in a jean jacket, who looked to be in his thirties, bounded on to the stage on the far side of the dance floor. "Hey, all, I'm Jammin' James Jupiter from your favorite oldies station, WQRN, right here in the Big Apple. We've got a special guest comin' on to sing for you tonight. She's not an oldie, but she sure is a goodie."

"Hey, we *are* getting live music!" Karma said happily, biting into a french fry.

"This talented lady just signed to do her first album with Warner Brothers, but here in the Big

Apple we've known about her talent for years. Put your hands together for . . . Mindy Moscow!"

Karma dropped her french fry.

"Wow!" Demetrius exclaimed. "What a great coincidence, huh?"

"Yeah, great," Karma agreed. "I'm beyond thrilled."

Mindy Moscow took the stage to enthusiastic applause.

She really is gorgeous, Karma thought reluctantly. *And she really does look like Kate Moss. Except with breasts.*

Mindy sat down at the black upright piano on the stage and leaned over to speak into the microphone. "Hi, everyone. I hope you don't mind my crashing your party."

"We love you, Mindy!" someone yelled out.

"Thanks," Mindy replied. "I guess that means I can stay. I'd like to play a new song that will be on my album—which I have to tell you, I'm really excited about. It's called *Tree House.* I hope you like it."

Mindy sang in her husky, bluesy voice. The song was all about her first love, and how loving him reminded her of the tree house her father had built for her when she was a little girl, safe and protected in his arms.

"Tree-house lover, you're my tree house."

The last smoky notes of the song hung in the air. Then the whole club burst into delighted applause.

Okay, so she's great, Karma thought reluctantly. *So she's beyond great. So what?*

"Nice song," she told Demetrius.

"Yeah," he said. Something was strange about his voice. He turned to Karma. "Come on, I'll introduce you to her."

"Oh, we don't have to do that now," she said hastily. "I mean—"

Demetrius was already out of the booth. Karma had no choice but to follow.

Mindy was standing to the side of the stage, talking to Jammin' James Jupiter. Demetrius tapped her on the shoulder. She turned around.

"Tree!" she screamed happily, and jumped into his arms. "I don't believe this! What are you doing here?"

"It's just a great coincidence," Demetrius said warmly.

"This is so great!" Mindy cried, hugging him again. She put her arm through Demetrius'. "James, this is Tree. He was my first love."

"Nice to meet you, man," James said, shaking Demetrius' hand. "How'd you ever give this lady up?"

Demetrius shrugged good-naturedly.

"So, Tree is short for Demetrius, huh?" James asked.

"My own private nickname," Mindy explained.

80

"Hey, James, you're wanted on the phone," someone called to the deejay.

"Back in a flash," James said, and hurried off.

"Mindy, I want you to meet Karma," Demetrius said, turning around to look for Karma.

"Yeah, I'm still here," Karma said brightly. She stepped forward. "Hi."

"This is Karma Kushner," he said, his arm around her shoulders.

"It's so nice to meet you," Mindy said. "Tree has told me a lot about you."

"Oh, great," Karma managed. "I've heard about you, too."

"Yeah, Tree and I go way back," Mindy mused nostalgically, her eyes shining at Demetrius. "Did you like the song?"

"It was terrific," Demetrius said.

Mindy laughed happily, and threw herself into Demetrius' arms again. "I just can't believe you're here! So, tell me what's going on!"

As Demetrius talked to Mindy, Karma tuned his voice out. Because her mind was filled with a terrible train of thought that she was certain was the truth.

Mindy calls Demetrius Tree, she thought. *As in tree house. As in tree-house lover. As in the song she just sang.*

That song was about him.

She still loves him.

And she wants him back.

6

Karma padded into the living room early the next afternoon—she and Demetrius had stayed out until two A.M.—and squinted blearily at a note she saw on the coffee table:

Karma—

We didn't have the guts to wake you, but it's ten now. We're going with Alan and Nick on a Circle Line boat tour of the city. Yes, it is incredibly touristy, but Alan swears it will be good material for his Great American Novel. We know how much you would have wanted to come on this with us, so we'll drop you a postcard in a bottle from below the Statue of Liberty. Or, if you are highly motivated, you might want to swim out to meet us there. We'll be looking for you. Carry a rubber ducky in case you need it.

Love,
US

Swim out to the Statue of Liberty to meet them? Karma thought. *Not this girl. That involves actual exercise.*

She yawned and peered at the clock. It was already one-thirty. Then she went into the kitchen, happy to see that someone had made coffee, and poured herself a cup. Then she grabbed the "Fashions of the Times" supplement section of the Sunday *New York Times* and curled up on the couch.

"Polka-dot hot pants?" she said out loud, studying the super-skinny model in the latest fashion. "Been there, done that." She turned the page and sipped her strong, black coffee.

The phone rang.

"It's Sunday!" she screamed at the phone. "Chelsea is off duty!"

The phone rang again. She reached over and snatched it up.

"Kushner Agency," she barked into it. "And whatever you want Chelsea to do, I'm charging you double. Don't you know it's Sunday?"

"Is this Karma?" a female voice asked uncertainly. "Karma Kushner?"

"I just said this is the Kushner Agency,"

Karma said, sure that it was simply some other media vulture looking to sink his or her teeth into Chelsea. "Who's this? And whaddaya want?"

"Karma, it's Muriel Cho. You sound . . . strange."

"I don't know any—"

Muriel Cho. Janelle's mother.

Whoa.

"Hi!" she said brightly. "I thought you were someone else! That is, I mean . . . never mind. So, Mrs. Cho. Hi!"

"Please, call me Muriel."

"Okay, Muriel," Karma replied. "This is . . . kind of a surprise. To hear from you, I mean."

"Yes, I realize that," Mrs. Cho said. "I found your phone number in Janelle's room. I hope you don't mind my calling you. Karma, do you have plans for this afternoon?"

"Not really," Karma admitted. "Why?"

"I'd like to take you to lunch."

Karma was stunned. "I thought you and your husband wanted to pretend I don't exist," she reminded Janelle's mother.

"I'm sure that hurt your feelings," Mrs. Cho said. "I'm sorry."

"It didn't hurt my feelings," Karma lied. "But it does make this phone call seem pretty weird."

"Yes, I can see how you'd feel that way. I . . . I can't really explain over the phone. My husband thinks I came into the city today to go shopping."

"Uh-huh," Karma said, even though she was utterly confused.

"I actually came into the city to try and see you," Mrs. Cho admitted. "Henry and Janelle have no idea that I'm not at Macy's buying a birthday present for my aunt."

"Mrs. Cho—"

"Muriel," the woman corrected Karma.

"Muriel, then," Karma said into the phone, "if you don't mind my saying so, you have a very secretive family."

"Yes, I suppose we do. So, may I take you to lunch? It would . . . mean a lot to me."

"I . . . yeah, I guess," Karma agreed.

"Where do you live?"

Karma told her.

"Is there a diner you usually go to?" Muriel asked. "I can meet you there."

"How about the place directly across from Lincoln Center, on Amsterdam Avenue?" Karma suggested, stunned by this turn of events. "I can meet you there in a half hour or so."

"Fine," Muriel agreed.

"Good," Karma said. "And Muriel?"

"Yes, Karma?"

"Muriel, don't change your mind."

Karma hung up. Then she did the world's quickest down-and-dirty makeup job on her face, pulled on a clean white T-shirt and some jeans, and pulled her hair back in a high pony-tail—there was no time to be her usual clotheshorse self. Then she left the apartment and quickly walked the several blocks over to the diner across from Lincoln Center, the famous performing arts center.

I hope I remember what she looks like, she thought as she approached the place. *I guess she knows just what I look like. Her daughter.*

Muriel Cho rose to her feet as Karma approached the table where she was sitting. She smiled. "In that outfit you really do look exactly like Janelle."

"Thanks . . . I guess." Karma took a seat opposite Mrs. Cho.

"This lunch never happened," Muriel said, sipping from the cup of coffee in front of her. "Do you understand?"

"Not really," Karma said honestly. "I don't understand any of this."

"I don't want them to know I met with you," Muriel explained.

"Yeah, I got that part," Karma replied. "Look, it's okay. It's not like I hang out with Janelle or anything. She won't even return my phone calls anymore."

She picked up the menu that lay on the table and studied it. When the waiter arrived, she ordered a pastrami sandwich and a cup of coffee. The coffee came quickly and she took a sip. "Did you already order?"

"I'm not hungry," the older woman said with

a small smile. She looked down at her coffee. "There's ... there's a lot that you don't know about Janelle," she said quietly.

"Yeah, well, there's a lot she doesn't know about me, either," Karma said. "And clearly she has no interest in knowing." She took another sip of coffee. "Mmmm, hot and black. It could be stronger, but it'll do."

Muriel smiled. "That's how Janelle drinks it, too."

"Quadruple bingo," Karma said, taking another sip of her coffee. "So, tell me some of the things that I don't know."

"You don't know that Janelle tapes your television show almost every day when she's home," Muriel said.

"No way," Karma replied.

"I always used to ask her why she taped that terrible show—I hope you'll forgive me," Muriel added quickly.

"It's okay," Karma said. "There's a reason that they call it *Trash*."

"Anyway, I never understood why she taped it. It's not the kind of thing she normally likes. She hardly watches television at all, and even then it's usually CNN. But now I understand why she tapes *Trash*."

"Maybe she's just a closet lover of trash TV," Karma suggested.

"No," Mrs. Cho said firmly. "I think she tapes it to see if you'll be on."

"Oh, I'm only an intern, I'm never on,"

Karma said. "Well, hardly ever. Anyway, if she wants a tape of me, I'll send her a videotape of my bat mitzvah. She can watch it over and over if she wants."

"You're Jewish?" Muriel asked, surprised.

"Wasn't the last name Kushner a big give-away for you?" Karma returned.

"I never thought about it," Mrs. Cho admitted. "You're Jewish."

"I just said that," Karma told her. "And you're—"

"Christian," Muriel said. "We go to the Korean Christian Church in Tenafly. Janelle goes with us every Sunday. In fact, last year she taught Sunday school, but this year she's too busy. That's another thing you didn't know about her."

"Cool," Karma said. "Tell me more."

"You tell me something she doesn't know about you," Muriel suggested as the waiter placed Karma's sandwich on the table in front of her.

"I have a subscription to *Business Week*," Karma said, taking a huge bite of her sandwich.

"So does Janelle."

"And *Barron's*."

"So does Janelle."

Karma put down her sandwich. "I bought call options on Compaq stock last week."

"So did she."

"This is a joke, right?" Karma asked.

"No joke," Mrs. Cho said. "It's incredible. Geneticists should study the two of you."

"Hey, I've got one where I bet we're different," Karma barked. "I flunked math!"

"Not Janelle." Muriel smiled as she spoke. "Not with me, a mathematics teacher."

"I would have disappointed you," Karma concluded, picking up her sandwich again.

"I doubt it," Muriel said. "So, any major medical problems?" she added casually.

"Yeah, and it's serious," Karma replied.

Muriel's face paled. "What is it?"

"I'm short," Karma stated. "Have you ever tried to find high fashion for the vertically challenged?"

Muriel smiled. "You have a lovely sense of humor."

"Thanks." She took another bite of her sandwich.

"No, really," Muriel asked, her face inquisitive. "Do you have any medical problems?"

Karma put down her sandwich again. "Why are you asking?"

"I'm just curious," Muriel said, her tone still casual. "I'm trying to get to know you better."

"As far as I know I am disgustingly healthy," Karma whined. "I don't drink and I don't smoke and I don't work out, but I love sugar."

"So does Janelle," Mrs. Cho said softly, looking down at her coffee. "Love sugar, I mean."

She raised her face to Karma. "Janelle has a

problem," Muriel said slowly. "A health problem. I wanted to tell you about it."

Karma felt a small shiver of fear. *What if it's some genetic thing?* she worried. *What if something is wrong with me, too?*

"I'm listening," she said, putting her sandwich down yet again.

"She only has one functioning kidney," Muriel explained. "She had a bad infection when she was a girl, and she lost the function of her other kidney."

"It isn't life threatening, is it?" Karma asked.

She vaguely recalled from the little attention she'd paid in high school biology that everyone was born with two kidneys, and that a person could live pretty normally with only one.

"No," Muriel answered. "Thank God. I don't know what Henry and I would do if we lost Janelle."

"Hopefully, you'll never have to find out." Karma reached for the last of her sandwich to polish it off.

Muriel took a sip of her coffee. "I hope you don't mind that I called you."

"No," Karma said. "Frankly, though, I would rather it had been Janelle."

"Maybe she'll change her mind," Mrs. Cho mused. "I think that would be very good. For both of you."

"Listen, are you sure that Janelle is okay?" Karma asked.

"She is fine," Mrs. Cho assured her. "I didn't mean to worry you."

Karma picked up the crumbs from her dish with her pinky. "I was wondering. You wouldn't know anything about my biological parents back in Korea. Would you?"

"What did your own mother tell you?" Mrs. Cho asked.

"She says they didn't tell her squat," Karma said. "And it's pretty clear they lied to both of you about our not having any siblings."

"That's true."

Karma looked at the older woman. "Why would an adoption agency do that?"

"I don't know," Mrs. Cho said. "Perhaps it was an honest mistake."

"Yeah, right," Karma scoffed. "Let's see. These two baby girls were born at exactly the same time and they look exactly like each other. And, hey, they have the same mother! Do you think they're twins? Nahhh."

Mrs. Cho laughed. "I have to say, you are much funnier than my daughter."

"Yeah, she didn't strike me as the laugh-a-minute type," Karma agreed. "Well, maybe that's a nurture thing, huh? There are some real hilarious characters in my family."

"That's nice," Mrs. Cho said. She looked at her watch.

"You really don't know anything about my birth family?" Karma asked again.

"Your birth mother—" Mrs. Cho began. And then she stopped herself.

"What?" Karma asked, excited. "I really want to know anything!"

"No, nothing," Muriel said quickly. "I don't know anything."

"Are you sure?" Karma pressed. "Because it seemed like you were about to—"

"No," Mrs. Cho said firmly. "I don't know anything." She looked at her watch again. "And now I have to fly. I'm glad I got to spend some time with you."

"Me, too," Karma said.

Mrs. Cho reached across the table and took her hand. "You are a lovely young lady, Karma."

"Yeah, I look just like your daughter," Karma joked.

"No, you're lovely on the inside," Muriel said. And then she smiled. "But that makes you like my daughter, too."

Muriel paid the cheek and left, and Karma decided to stay and have dessert.

That was one weird conversation, she thought. *Call me crazy, but I have a feeling she's keeping something from me. Something about my birth mother.*

And it isn't something good.

Karma let herself into the apartment, still thinking about everything that Mrs. Cho had told her. After she had finished dessert, she'd gone to Central Park, where she'd laid in the sun and thought about her life.

It's all just so strange, she had mused. *I love my parents and I love my life. But what if they had adopted the other twin? I'd be this Christian girl living in Teaneck. Muriel would be my mother.*

It's all just random luck, I guess. Or, as my parents say, karma.

Who the heck knows what it is.

After lolling in the sun for a couple of hours, she walked back to the apartment, still wondering about how and why her life had turned out the way it had.

I just have this feeling that Muriel is keeping something from me, Karma thought for the zillionth time as she entered the elevator in her building. *Why did she suddenly want to take me to lunch? Why did she ask me about my health?*

"Oh, hi," Chelsea said breathlessly, scrambling up from the couch as Karma came in. Lying underneath where she had been lying was Nick, with a huge grin on his face.

"Hi, yourself," Karma responded. "Sorry to interrupt, but isn't that why God created bedrooms?"

"We were just talking." Nick yawned, stretching his hands over his head.

"Oh, yeah, and I was just lunching with the pope," Karma scoffed. She sat in the overstuffed chair. "I'm really glad you two decided to make up."

94

"So am I." Chelsea lifted Nick's legs and sat under them. "So, where were you?"

"You're not going to believe this," Karma said, and then she told them.

"Wow," Chelsea breathed when Karma had concluded her story. "That's really strange."

"Tell me about it." Karma shrugged. "So, how was the Circle Line?" she asked.

"Fun," Chelsea said. "Except for when this Boy Scout troop recognized me. I wore a baseball cap and dark sunglasses, but it didn't help."

"All those little boys lusting after you," Nick teased. "You loved it."

"I did not," Chelsea insisted, blushing.

"Soon you'll be rich enough to own your own yacht," Karma pointed out. "No more Circle Line with the unwashed masses."

"I still haven't decided about doing the book," Chelsea said.

"Take all the time you need," Karma instructed her. "But as your agent, I have to say—"

"Don't push me, please," Chelsea begged.

There was a knock on the door.

"Anyone expecting anyone?" Nick asked them.

"Antoine didn't buzz us," Karma said, going to the door. She looked through the peephole. "It's Alan." She opened the door.

"Hey, Karma," Alan said.

"Come on in."

"You'll never guess who's over at our apartment right now," Alan said as he walked in.

"Jazz?" Chelsea guessed, joking around.

"How did you know?" Alan looked at her, astounded.

"I was kidding!" Chelsea cried. "Is she, really?"

"She is," Alan said. "She just showed up. And guess who she's looking for." He looked pointedly at Nick.

"Aw, man," Nick groaned. "It's Sunday. She doesn't own my butt until nine o'clock tomorrow morning."

"I'd like to think I can do anything with your butt any time," Jazz interjected from the doorway. She wore faded jeans and a denim bra top. She walked into the apartment, looking around. "Well, isn't this quaint. We rented you a nice place."

"I'm busy, Jazz," Nick said from his place on the couch.

"I can see that," Jazz returned. She wandered over to the bad erotic art on the wall and looked at it. "This painting is awful."

"It came with the apartment," Karma explained.

"Uh-huh," Jazz murmured.

"So . . . would you like a drink?" Karma offered.

"She isn't staying," Nick said.

"I'd love a drink, Karma," Jazz said. "Thank you."

"How about a beer?" Nick asked slyly.

"But you know I can't drink beer now," Jazz responded. "After all, I'm pregnant."

"How could we possibly forget?" Nick asked.

Jazz leaned against the wall and folded her arms. "You know, it really isn't polite to let a pregnant woman stand when you're lying all over the couch."

Nick lifted his legs from Chelsea and they both got up. Jazz sat down. Karma got Jazz a Coke and handed it to her.

"This is so nice," Jazz commented, sipping the Coke. "Gee, I seem to have read somewhere that Coke isn't good to drink when you're pregnant, either. I'll have to look into that." She took a small sip of her drink.

"So, Jazz," Alan began, "we weren't expecting you."

"True," Jazz agreed. "But you have to admit, it's a nice surprise, right?"

"Sure," Karma managed.

"So, I was thinking," Jazz continued. "My limo is waiting downstairs. Why don't we all go out and have some fun?"

"I have to change to go to work," Karma said.

"Too bad," Jazz murmured. "Okay, how about the four of us, then?"

"I have a date," Alan said. "With Lisha."

"Oh." Jazz turned to Nick and Chelsea. "Well, I guess it'll just be the three of us, then, huh?"

"Listen, Jazz, I really don't want to—" Chelsea began.

"Oh, come on." Jazz pouted as she spoke. "After all, you're a big celebrity now. And everyone knows Nick and I . . . well, you know. Now, can you imagine how the flashbulbs will be going off when the three of us show up together?"

"No, thanks," Chelsea said coldly. "I'm really not interested."

"Too bad," Jazz concluded crisply, and stood up. "Nick?"

He just stared at her.

"Well, can't say I didn't try," Jazz said easily. She walked to the door, then turned back to the group. "Oh, by the way, I'm planning to announce who the father of my baby is soon. Very soon," she added, looking right at Nick.

"Very, very soon, indeed."

And then she walked out the door.

"**I** do not want to do this," Karma told her roommates, as she nervously pawed through her closet. "I have nothing to wear."

It was the next evening, and Karma had agreed to go on a double date with Demetrius, Mindy Moscow, and the guy Mindy was dating. Demetrius was due to pick her up in fifteen minutes, and she was still standing in her bedroom in her underwear.

"*You* have nothing to wear?" Lisha echoed, laughter in her voice. She was lolling on Karma's bed, her head propped up with three pillows. Chelsea lay on her stomach next to Lisha, her feet swinging in the air.

"Nothing feels right," Karma complained. She pulled a yellow T-shirt dress by a hip, new designer out of her closet. "Yuck." She dropped it on the floor.

"You can't really be insecure about Mindy," Lisha said.

"Why not?" Karma asked, her head disappearing into her closet again. She pulled out a striped tube dress, very short, in a slinky material. "What about this?"

"It's cute," Chelsea commented.

"Nah, I'll look like a cocktail frank," Karma decided, adding the dress to the growing pile of clothes on the floor.

"So go naked," Lisha suggested. "It's a good look for you."

Karma looked at her profile in the mirror over her dresser. "Maybe I need those silicone things you put in your bra to make it look like you have cleavage."

"Karma, come on," Chelsea groaned.

"Mindy has great cleavage," Karma said darkly.

"But Demetrius isn't with Mindy," Lisha reminded Karma. "He's with you."

Karma's head dove into her closet again. She pulled out a hot-pink sundress and held it up to herself. "Well?"

"Cute," Chelsea decreed. "Put it on."

Karma pulled it over her head. Then she rummaged through the floor of her closet until she found some apple-green-and-hot-pink strappy sandals, with very high, chunky heels. She put them on and turned to her friends.

"Yeah?" she asked.

"Yeah," Lisha said firmly.

Karma looked at herself in the mirror again. "I don't know."

Her friends groaned.

"I need more eyeliner," Karma decided. She quickly relined her eyes, then filled her lips in with a pale beige lipstick from her favorite cosmetics line, M.A.C. She was spraying herself with perfume when the intercom buzzed.

"It's Demetrius," she yelped. "Maybe this outfit is too—"

"I can't believe this is the Karma Kushner I know and love." Lisha shook her head in exasperation as she got up to buzz Demetrius in.

"I'm obsessing, huh?" Karma said sheepishly.

Chelsea nodded.

"Okay, I'll stop," Karma announced. "It's so tacky, right?"

Chelsea nodded again.

"Right," Karma agreed. "I'm way too cool to obsess just because my boyfriend and I are going out with his ex. Who is really cute. And talented. And famous."

"He's on his way up!" Lisha called in to them.

Karma panicked. "Maybe this outfit is too—"

"Forget it!" Chelsea cried, jumping off the bed. "Go out there and knock him dead, girl!"

"I wish you'd hurry up and take the book deal so I can say I have a best friend—and client— who's a millionaire," Karma groused. "It helps my self-confidence."

"That doesn't seem like a good enough reason to do it," Chelsea pointed out. "You know what's so strange? How Jazz was actually nice to me at work today."

"Sure," Karma said, adding some blush to her cheeks. "For the moment you're more famous than she is. She didn't bargain for that, you know. She thought she'd have you totally under her thumb with this stunt. Ha!"

"Karma, Mr. Studly is here!" Lisha called.

Karma and Chelsea went into the living room.

"Hi," Demetrius said. "You look great."

"Told ya," Lisha said smugly.

"Thanks," Karma said. "So, let's go. We're meeting them there, right?"

They had planned on going to a new coffee-house. Mindy would be performing there the following week.

"Actually, Mindy is downstairs in the taxi," Demetrius said. "I had it wait."

"How'd that happen?" Karma asked.

"It was funny," Demetrius answered. "She happened to be in my neighborhood, so she buzzed me and we came over here together."

"She just happened to be in your neighborhood?" Karma asked dubiously.

"Yeah," Demetrius said easily.

"Where's her date?" Karma asked.

"She says he's got the flu."

"Gee, too bad." Karma's voice was flat.

Demetrius didn't seem to notice. "So, let's go. The meter is running on the taxi."

"Have fun, you two," Lisha called out.

"Have a blast," Chelsea added.

"Thanks," Karma said. "It's going to be . . . an experience."

I'd rather be having a root canal, she thought as she and Demetrius rode down the elevator together.

You can't tell me Mindy didn't plan this whole thing. She probably never had a date tonight at all. There probably isn't even a boyfriend in the picture.

Of course not.

Because Mindy wants my boyfriend.

"So, Karma, tell me all about yourself," Mindy said warmly, after the waitress took their orders.

Even though it was a Monday night, the coffeehouse was crowded and smoky. Alternative music blasted from the sound system. The wooden tables were all covered in white butchershop paper, with a bowl of crayons in the center of each table.

"Oh, there's not much to tell," Karma said, idly picking out a bright red crayon.

Mindy smiled. "I doubt that." She put her hand on Demetrius' arm. "If Tree likes you, you must be very special."

Karma drew a little hangman with her red crayon. To the stick figure she added Mindy's hair and two circles to represent breasts. "That's so sweet of you to say," she oozed.

She drew a little thought circle above Mindy's head, and wrote HELP ME!! in the bubble.

"You work at *Trash,* right?" Mindy asked.

Karma put her crayon down and smiled at Mindy. "Right."

"It must be fun, huh?"

"Yeah, a blast," she agreed, then looked over at Demetrius. Mindy still had her hand on his arm.

"You're quiet," Karma observed.

"I'm just really enjoying having the two of you here," he said.

And I would really enjoy giving you a fat lip, Karma thought. *Why don't you tell her to get her hand off your arm, huh?*

"You're just as sweet as ever, Tree," Mindy said warmly. "Isn't he the sweetest guy?" she asked Karma.

"The sweetest," Karma agreed, her voice flat.

"It's just . . . there are so many insincere people in this world," Mindy continued. "And it's nice to know that a guy like Tree actually exists."

"Excuse me," an attractive blond-haired guy with an earring said, stopping at their table, his eyes on Mindy. "But aren't you Mindy Moscow?"

"That's right," Mindy replied.

"I think you're awesome," the guy said. "I mean it."

"Thanks," Mindy said easily. "I appreciate that."

"So, I heard you got signed to Warner, huh?" the guy asked.

"Right," Mindy confirmed. "I'll be going into the studio to record next month."

"Awesome," the guy said again. "I'll buy your CD as soon as it comes out. I heard you sing at

Molten Java. I really liked that song 'Tree House.'"

"Thanks," Mindy replied, looking over at Demetrius. "It's very special to me."

"Good luck with your album!" the guy said, and he walked away.

"I guess that happens to you a lot, huh?" Karma asked.

"Sometimes," Mindy said. "It means so much to me, you know? That people appreciate my music."

"Well, your music is great," Karma told her sincerely.

The waitress set their mugs of coffee on the table. Karma's covered the little drawing of Mindy she'd made.

"So, what did you think of 'Tree House'?" Mindy asked Demetrius as she poured sugar into her coffee.

"I told you the other night," he said. He sounded uncomfortable.

Mindy looked at Karma. "I wrote that song for Tree."

"Duh," Karma replied.

Mindy laughed. "Okay, I guess you're right. It was obvious."

"Once I heard you call him Tree for the seventy-fifth time, I had an inkling," Karma said, sipping her coffee.

"You don't mind, do you?" Mindy asked.

"Why would I mind?" Karma asked back. "Hey,

I'm kind of hungry." She looked around for the waitress. "I think I'll order dessert."

"Mindy Moscow!" a tall, thin woman cried, running over to their table. "You're Mindy Moscow, right?"

"Right," Mindy answered.

"You are my son's favorite singer in the world," the woman declared. "We're sitting right over there, and it's his birthday. Would you mind terribly just coming over so I could get a photo of the two of you together? It would mean the world to him, but he's too shy to ask."

"Sure," Mindy said graciously. She stood up. "Be right back."

"Gee, it must be rough, being so gorgeous and talented and famous," Karma whined.

"And she hasn't even had an album out yet," Demetrius agreed. "It's amazing that she has such a huge following already."

Karma sipped her coffee. "So."

"Are you having fun?" Demetrius asked.

"Oh, sure," she lied. "It's just lovely . . . *Tree,*" she added pointedly.

Demetrius had the grace to look chagrined. "Does that bother you?"

"Not at all," Karma replied coolly.

"I could ask her to stop calling me that," he offered. "I mean, it would be strange, since she's always called me that."

"Oh, well then, I wouldn't want to deprive you of your little nickname," Karma said.

"You're upset."

"Brilliant deduction," Karma remarked.

"Karma, Mindy and I are just friends now."

"According to you, maybe," Karma said. "According to her, the two of you are about to climb back into the ol' tree house and go at it."

"Where did you get that from?"

"Because I have eyes," Karma said. "She wants you back."

"Karma, that is ridiculous," Demetrius said flatly. "She's seeing this new guy—"

"So where is he, then?"

"He got the flu—"

"He doesn't exist," Karma stated. "And even if he did exist, that wouldn't mean that she doesn't want you back."

Demetrius took a sip of his coffee. "Maybe this double date wasn't a great idea."

Karma didn't reply.

"I just thought . . . look, there's nothing wrong with being friends with your ex," Demetrius said defensively. "I care about her."

"Like in what way?" Karma asked.

"I told you," Demetrius answered. "She's my friend."

"How close a friend?"

"It isn't like that, Karma."

Karma leaned closer to him. "What, are you telling me that you have totally no sexual or romantic feelings for her anymore? At all? Can you look me in the eye and tell me that?"

"Yes," Demetrius replied calmly. "I can."

Wow, I almost believe him, Karma thought, looking into the two dark pools of his eyes.

She sat back. "Well, that doesn't mean she feels the same way you do."

"Karma . . ." Demetrius reached out to stroke her cheek. "It doesn't matter what she feels."

"It doesn't?"

"No." He leaned over and kissed her.

"The problem is that she's really nice," Karma admitted. "I mean, I'd like to hate her, but I can't."

"If you'd get over being jealous, you'd actually like her," Demetrius said.

Karma picked up her coffee. "I'm not jealous."

He leaned over and kissed her again. "Good."

She tugged on a lock of his long hair. "You're kind of cute, you know. I might just keep you." She got up from the table. "Excuse me, the ladies' room calls."

Karma wound her way through the packed tables until she found the ladies' room at the back of the club. She pushed the wooden door open and went in.

And there was Mindy, standing in front of the mirror, brushing her hair.

Okay, so she's gorgeous, Karma thought reluctantly. *And she looks great in those jeans and that tiny, little black jacket. Very downtown hip.*

"Karma, hi!" Mindy said.

"Hi." Karma went into the stall to pee, came out, and washed her hands. Mindy was still at the mirror, putting on some lip gloss.

"My lips get so chapped, even in the summer," Mindy remarked.

"Uh-huh," Karma replied, drying her hands under the air dryer.

Mindy dropped her lip gloss into her little purse and turned to Karma. "I want you to know how lucky you are. To have Tree, I mean."

"He's lucky, too," Karma replied. She looked into the mirror and adjusted the bottom of her short dress.

"He is," Mindy agreed. "You are really beautiful."

"Me?" Karma squeaked, totally taken by surprise. "I was just thinking that about you!"

"Really?" Mindy said, laughing.

"Really," Karma admitted.

"Well, thanks, I'm very flattered," Mindy said. "And I want to tell you how nice I think it is, your willingness to let me come out with you guys."

"It was supposed to be a double date," Karma reminded her.

Mindy shrugged. "I lied."

"I know," Karma told her. "You wanted to check me out."

Mindy smiled. "What gave me away?"

"It doesn't matter." Karma gestured dismissively, then leaned against the wall. "What I'd like to know, though, is, why? I mean, you must have a ton of guys after you."

"Not guys like Tree," Mindy said, shrugging again. "I got spoiled by the best."

"So if you feel like that, why did you break up with him?" Karma asked.

Mindy smiled sadly. "I ask myself that all the time." She slung the strap of her purse over her shoulder. "But you have nothing to worry about, Karma. We're just friends now. And he's totally into you. I'm not out to break you guys up."

Yeah. Like I really believe that, Karma thought.

"You ready to go back to the table?" Mindy asked.

"Sure."

Mindy turned back to Karma. "Listen, Karma, I really like you. And I apologize for telling a little white lie to get the three of us together tonight. Forgive me?"

"It's not a big deal," Karma replied.

"Good." Mindy gave her a bright smile. "You're a sweetheart. And if there's anything I can ever do for you, just ask." She opened the door to the ladies' room.

"There is something you can do for me, actually," Karma said.

"What's that?"

"Stop calling Demetrius Tree," she said bluntly.

"But I've always called him—"

Karma gave her a jaded look.

"I'll try," Mindy promised.

"Try hard," Karma urged her. And then she swept past Mindy and returned to the table.

8

"Up, up, up, sweetheart!" Karma called to Chelsea, thrusting a mug of coffee at her. "Let's rise and shine like Scarlett O'Hara, you famous Southern belle, you."

Chelsea looked sleepily at her, and then at her bedside clock radio.

"Karma," she croaked, "it's *six-thirty* in the morning. What day is it?"

"Tuesday," Karma said. "Good-news day." She held the coffee mug out in front of her friend until she took it.

"What are you doing?"

"Up first, then I'll explain," Karma told her. "Up, up, up!"

"Why are you completely dressed?" Chelsea asked, taking the coffee, finally, from her friend, and raising it to her lips. "We don't have to be at work until nine."

"Okay, you're officially awake," Karma an-

111

nounced. "Now get up, get dressed, and meet me in the living room in, oh, forty-five."

"Karma, have you lost your mind?"

"Big meeting this morning, Chelsea. Big meeting. I'm out here busting my butt, working for you—for us—and you're asking me if I've lost my mind?"

Chelsea lay back down on the bed. "I'm not going anywhere or doing anything until you explain. Because I really think you've lost it."

"Ah, you don't trust your agent," Karma countered. "Always trust your agent, Chelsea."

Actually, Karma had not lost her mind. In fact, she'd been up since five that morning, in the living room, making phone calls.

One of those phone calls had been to Lew Ricorda, publisher at Sunnybrook Books. She'd called him at the home number he'd given her during one of their earlier conversations, and definitely woken him up.

But Lew didn't seem to care. Especially when Karma told him that she and Chelsea wanted to meet with him, face-to-face, in his offices, at precisely seven forty-five that morning.

Oh yeah, and would Lew please arrange for a limo to pick the two of them up at their building and bring them to Sunnybrook Books headquarters at Avenue of the Americas and Fifty-fourth Street? And would that identical limo please wait down on the street until the meeting was over, and then bring Chelsea to the *Trash* offices at nine o'clock?

And I conveniently forgot to tell Lew that I, Karma Kushner, of the Karma Kushner Agency, am but a lowly intern at Trash.

"Can do," Lew had told Karma. "You're sure she'll meet with me?"

"Absolutely," Karma had said, though Chelsea was entirely unaware at this time of any meeting. "In fact, she insists on it."

"Great," Lew said. "I'll have coffee and Danish for us."

"Lemme give you an inside tip, Lew," Karma had finished. "Make the coffee beans Jamaican. That's what Chelsea drinks. And she likes Equal, not Sweet'n Low. Equal. Okay Lew, see you then. Bye."

A female editor in her mid-twenties, with longish brown hair and a matching longish nose, dressed reasonably hip in an apricot linen pantsuit, was waiting in the lobby at the huge office tower of which Sunnybrook Books occupied the fifteenth through the twenty-second floors.

"Chelsea Jennings!" she gushed, when Karma and Chelsea arrived in the lobby. She ran over to Chelsea and shook her hand profusely. "We're so pleased to welcome you to Sunnybrook Books. I'm Regina Hartzell."

Chelsea shook her hand politely. "Nice to meet you, Regina."

"Who's your friend?" Regina said, eyeing Karma warily.

113

"I'm Kushner," Karma said abruptly. "Karma Kushner. Her agent. *Agent.*"

"Really?" Regina asked. "But you look so young to be—"

"The head of Art Line Films is twenty-nine," Karma barked. "The new CEO of Prago Records is twenty-eight. They're both over the hill. Now, if we could just cut this love fest short, take us upstairs so we can get this day moving. We've got a *million* appointments. A million."

Chelsea bit her lip to keep from laughing and Karma rolled her eyes behind Regina's back as the young woman hurriedly led them to the elevator.

Regardless of what happens, Karma thought, *this is a ton of fun. Maybe I really do need to rethink my career path.*

Five minutes later Regina had guided Karma and Chelsea through the warren of cubicles that made up the twenty-first floor of the building, to a large corner office that belonged to Lew Ricorda.

"Right through that open door," Regina told them. "He's waiting for you inside. Is there anything I can get you?"

"Coffee black," Karma said. "Decent coffee."

"Oh, I already arranged that," Regina assured her. "It's waiting for you in Lew's office."

"Good," Karma said. "We'll see you later, Regina. Keep that limo waiting."

"Absolutely!" Regina replied. "In fact, I'll go right back downstairs to watch it for you."

"You do that," Karma instructed.

Regina hurried off.

"This may be the most fun I've ever had," Karma whispered to Chelsea.

The two of them cracked up together, then composed themselves quickly to meet Lew. They walked into the office.

"Chelsea? Karma? I'm Lew Ricorda. Welcome to Sunnybrook."

Lew Ricorda was a short, muscular man in his forties, with thick black hair and a surprisingly handsome face. If he was taken aback that Chelsea Jennings was being represented by a tiny eighteen-year-old Asian-American agent, he portrayed none of it.

Instead, he welcomed the two of them into his spacious office. Along one side, there was a rolling cart, on top of which were two coffee carafes, an assortment of mugs and cups, a clear pitcher filled with orange juice, and a serving tray that held fifteen or twenty different Danishes and doughnuts.

"Look," Chelsea said softly to Karma, pointing to the other side of the room. Karma followed her gaze as Lew looked on expectantly.

Karma's eyes panned around the room and stopped at a table.

On the table was a pyramid of thick, hardbound books, each of which had an identical, smartly designed, fabulous-looking cover.

FROM TRAGEDY TO TRIUMPH TO TRASH *TO TOMOR-ROW,* the title read, in big block letters. Under it was the line, *My story, by Chelsea Jennings.*

"Wow," Chelsea breathed. She walked over to the stack of books, picked one up, and turned it around so she could see the back cover. There, she saw a small, tasteful photograph of herself, along with some lines of dummy copy so that she could imagine more easily what the layout would finally look like.

"You like?" Lew asked her.

"It's incredible," Chelsea admitted.

"Interesting," Karma commented simply.

"I had our art department work all weekend on that for you, Chelsea," Lew informed her. "Of course, you'll have final approval on the design."

Karma saw Chelsea turn the book around and around in her hands.

"Won't the two of you sit down?" Lew asked politely. "Do you want something to eat?"

"Coffee," Karma barked, taking a seat on Lew's leather couch. "She takes Equal, no milk. Me, black."

Lew quickly got them their coffee, then he sat opposite them in an oversized brown leather chair. Conveniently placed on the coffee table in between them was another mock-up copy of *From Tragedy to Triumph to* Trash *to Tomorrow.* Lew picked it up and looked at it almost reverently.

"So you two see," he said, "we're planning to do this right."

"We haven't agreed to do this at all," Karma reminded him, sipping her coffee. She turned to Chelsea. "I think I liked the art mock-up better at—well, I'd rather not say which house it is. What do you think?"

A muscle in Lew's cheek jumped. "What other house would that be?"

"Oh, I'm not free to discuss that, Lew," Karma said.

Chelsea nodded.

Karma leaned forward and put her coffee on the table. "Lew, time to get down and dirty here. Lemme tell you what we're going to need to take this deal to the next level."

"Go," Lew said.

"A million-five to start," Karma told him, leaning forward on the couch. "Two-fifty bonus if it hits the best-seller list, two-fifty more if it goes to number one."

The chief exec of Sunnybrook Books just sat there, listening.

I can't believe he hasn't thrown both of us out of his office, Karma thought giddily. *This is too amazing.*

She plunged on.

"Two-fifty more if she does *Oprah,* a five-hundred bonus if we decide to let it go to film, plus the editor of our choice, plus a hundred for each printing."

Lew whistled, and smiled. "You drive a hard bargain, Karma."

"Thank you, Lew," Karma said calmly. "Call me Miss Kushner."

Lew laughed. "You should be working for me."

"No." Karma said, picking up her coffee again. "*You* should be working for *me*."

Lew Ricorda looked at her, and laughed again. "So, Chelsea," he said, "have we got a deal on your agent's terms?"

"Nah, nah, nah, Lew," Karma interrupted. "We aren't talking handshake yet."

"Why not?" Lew asked. "If I'm willing to agree to your terms. And I am."

"You *are*?" Karma was so shocked, she allowed her agent persona to slip for a moment.

"I am," Lew told her, then turned to Chelsea. "Is it a deal?"

Chelsea took a long look at Karma before she answered. Karma had just made a deal for her that could amount to well over two million dollars. And all she had to do was write the story of her life.

Karma and Lew both stared at her.

"I need a little more time." she finally said.

Lew looked at her closely. "How much more time?"

"I . . . I . . ." Chelsea stammered.

"Forty-eight hours," Karma answered for her.

Lew got a hard look in his eyes. "That's a firm offer I just made. Don't play games with me. Got that?"

"Got it." Karma nodded.

"Forty-eight hours," Lew said, standing up. "That's it."

"Agreed." Karma stood up, too. So did Chelsea.

Lew put his hand out to Karma. "You drive a hard bargain, Miss Kushner."

"Thanks, Lew," Karma said, shaking his hand. "And now we have a limo waiting."

The meeting was over.

"Two million *dollars*?" Alan asked incredulously.

"Yep," Karma confirmed.

All six interns were in Sicko-Central, transcribing phone calls to the 900 number. The number of calls had tripled since Jazz had announced her pregnancy and outted Chelsea on the air.

"Amazing." He took off his headphones and rubbed his sore ears. "Karma, you're in the wrong biz."

"True," Karma said. "And if Chelsea takes the deal, I will be more than two hundred thousand dollars richer."

Lisha looked over at Chelsea. "So, are you going to take it?"

Chelsea shrugged.

"That's a Lisha shrug," Nick remarked.

"Yeah," Sky agreed. "She uses it to mean don't-get-too-close."

"I do not," Lisha said.

"Yeah, you do," Sky insisted.

"You annoy me," Lisha told him.

"Now, kids, kids," Nick chided them, pretending to be their parent. "Play nice."

"She has until Thursday to decide," Karma continued. "So what's your vote, take it or leave it?"

"It's not up to them," Chelsea pointed out. "It's up to me."

"You don't want to know what your best friends think?" Lisha asked.

"I suppose I do," Chelsea admitted. "I'm just being obnoxious."

"You're stressed," Alan told her. "It makes sense. This whole thing is really stressful for you. And if you took the deal, it would change your whole life. And not for the better. Which is why I vote leave it."

"I say take it," Lisha said. "You'd be crazy to turn it down, Chels."

"I abstain," said Nick.

"You can't abstain," Lisha objected.

"I just did," Nick replied.

"I say take it," Karma said. "How can she turn it down?"

"Easy," Alan answered. "Look, my parents are . . . well, they're kind of rich, okay? And believe me, it doesn't make them happy. Our house is a war zone."

"That doesn't mean it won't make Chelsea happy," Lisha pointed out.

"What about the ethics of it?" Sky asked.

"She'd be making money off of what her father did."

"Well, she didn't do it," Lisha said.

"So?" Sky went on. "That doesn't make it right to take money for—"

"So she could give half of it to charity if she wanted to," Lisha cut in. "Then she'd still be rich and she would have done some good, too. What about that?"

"I don't think so," Alan said. "Because is she—"

"Y'all, this is not helpful," Chelsea called out over their voices. "I mean, I appreciate your thoughts, but . . . I just need some quiet." She pulled her earphones back on.

Karma looked up at the clock. It was late afternoon, almost time for *Trash* to start.

From super-agent to lowly intern in one day, she thought, pushing the pause button on her tape. *What a life.*

Karma put her elbows on the desk in front of her and began to daydream about Demetrius. After they dropped Mindy off the night before, they had gone down to the Hudson River and walked along the pier. It had been so romantic. And then they'd stopped to kiss. And the kisses had lasted until just three hours before Karma woke up Chelsea.

I am so crazy about him, Karma thought. *It can be dangerous to be so crazy about a guy.*

And then a strange thought popped into her head. *I wonder if Janelle has a boyfriend.*

Karma shook her head and turned to Lisha at the next desk. "Could you please tell me how my life got so complicated?"

"You love it," Lisha told her.

"Yeah," Karma admitted. "Kinda."

The monitor was on, the volume turned down low, and Karma looked up at it. Jazz was giving an update on a show she'd done some time ago in which *Trash* had decided to give an all-expenses-paid full plastic-surgery makeover to the most obnoxious person they could find.

Now Karma could see on the screen that Jazz was showing videotape of the person they'd chosen actually undergoing plastic surgery.

"Turn it up," Karma urged Sky, who was closest to the monitor. "I have to hear this."

Sky obliged.

"Liposuction, new nose, lips, chin, dermabrasion, hair weaving," Jazz said. "By the end of the summer, we'll have a new woman here! And we'll bring her back on for you, gang."

"Gee, I'm really looking forward to that show," Sky said sarcastically.

"As far as I'm concerned," Alan declared, "the world was far better off before people started going under the knife because they didn't happen to like their looks."

"I don't see anything wrong with it," Lisha put in mildly.

"But there is," Alan maintained. "In a hundred years we'll be a nation of little plastic cookie-cutter people walking around. There happen to be many different kinds of beauty. You don't have to be thin and blond to be beautiful."

"Yeah, tell that to my thighs," Lisha muttered.

"Man, we need to resurrect the Trash-cam," Nick suggested, staring at Jazz on the monitor.

"We can set it up again soon," Sky said. They'd were referring to the tiny hidden video camera that the interns had been using to record material for their *My TRASHy Summer* underground video.

They'd been laying low for a while with it after a scary incident in Jazz's office when they'd almost got caught, but lately they'd been talking about setting it up again.

"I want it in Barry's office," Lisha said. "He spends too much time in there alone."

"Or with Bigfoot," Sky added.

"Well, we already know what they're doing together," Lisha said with a snort. "And it ain't exactly work."

"I don't know," Alan joked. "As far as I'm concerned, having sex with Bigfoot *would be* work."

They all cracked up.

"I wish we could just put it in Jazz's doctor's office," Alan said. "Then we'd know the truth."

Karma snuck a look over at Nick, who was looking at Chelsea as she took off her earphones to watch Jazz.

"And now, gang, I have a big announcement," Jazz was saying on the monitor.

The number-one camera came in tight on Jazz's stomach.

Nick paled.

"Well, gang," Jazz said, "we've got a projected due date for the kid!"

Everyone in the studio cheered, knowing exactly what she was talking about.

"What is it, Jazz?" someone in the studio yelled out.

"The date, or the kid?" Jazz shot back. "Well, let's take a poll. Who says it's a boy?"

Pandemonium.

"Who says it's a girl?"

More pandemonium.

"Who says it's twin girls, and I'm going to name them *both* Jazz?"

Absolute pandemonium.

The camera closed in even tighter on Jazz. The studio quieted.

"I know you all have been wondering who the father of my child is," Jazz said. "Well, I want to tell you."

"Oh, God," Chelsea whispered.

Nick put his hand to his forehead. He looked sick.

"But first," Jazz continued, "I want to thank you guys for all the cool stuff you've been sending for the baby. It's unreal!"

The audience applauded.

"So, this is the moment you've been waiting for," Jazz resumed. "You all deserve to know, because we're all in this trashy world together, right?"

"Right!" the studio audience yelled.

The camera moved in on Jazz's face. "The father of my kid is . . . oh, looks like we're out of time!"

The audience yelled and catcalled their disapproval.

"What, you think I tricked you?" Jazz asked. "Teased you? Made you want to watch again on, say . . . Friday, when I announce the guy's name?" She smiled. "What can I tell you? It's a trashy world out there. And I like being the trashiest of them all. You know what I say. . . ."

"How trashy it is!" the whole audience yelled with her.

"Bye, gang, see you tomorrow!"

The credits started to roll.

"She amazes me," Lisha murmured.

"My life is a soap opera," Chelsea said, shaking her head.

"I know the feeling." Karma stood up and stretched. "At least it isn't boring, huh?

Her friends laughed.

"Just think, Chels, by the end of the week, you could be a multimillionaire."

"A multimillionaire whose mother isn't speaking to her and whose boyfriend might be announced as the father of Jazz's baby," Chelsea added.

"Well, yeah," Karma agreed. "Your life *is* a little complicated."

"And I'm *not* the father of Jazz's baby," Nick put in.

"You don't know that for sure," Alan pointed out, leaning back in his chair.

"Hey, man," Nick began heatedly, "the odds of—"

"Don't fight, you two," Sky interrupted.

This is about Chelsea, Karma realized. *Alan is jealous. Wow. I hope I wasn't that transparent last night with Mindy.*

"Look, you guys, let's forget about all this stuff and plan something," Karma suggested. "I know. Let's go out to dinner together tonight."

"I'm busy," Alan said.

"Me, too," Sky added.

"I have a headache," Chelsea said.

"And I'm broke," Lisha put in. "Some of us don't have million-dollar offers for our life story on the table."

"Hey, we can't let all this crap come between us!" Karma cried.

No one answered her.

"What happened to how all six of us are in this together?" she asked them.

No one answered.

Great, Karma thought. *Just great. Money and jealousy are coming between the six of us.*

What if it breaks us up forever?

"Anyone hungry?" Karma called, coming into the kitchen. She looked at the clock on the wall. It was eight o'clock and she hadn't eaten anything since the candy bar she'd scarfed at three.

"The concept of meals has no meaning to me," Lisha said from the couch, where she lay, sprawled out, reading a book. "I feed my face twenty-four hours a day lately. My thighs are getting way too intimate with each other."

"Chels? You hungry?" Karma asked.

Chelsea was sitting on the rug, staring at the phone. She didn't answer.

"Chels?" Karma asked again.

"I can't think about food now," she answered. "I'm willing the phone to ring."

"Nick?" Karma guessed, going to the refrigerator.

"My mother," Chelsea said. "I finally got

through to her. She said she was on the other line and she'd call me back."

"Well, that's progress," Karma remarked, poking her head into the fridge. She found a hunk of moldy cheese, some wilted lettuce, and some vitamins. "None of us went grocery shopping, I see."

"If I buy it, I eat it." Lisha didn't bother to look up from her book.

"Lish, please, don't get all crazed about your weight," Karma begged.

"I know I've gained weight," Lisha said darkly. "My jeans are tight."

"You wear your jeans tight," Karma pointed out. She opened the cupboard and found a bag of pretzels. There were only two in the bottom of the bag.

"If I get fat again like I used to be, I will die," Lisha announced.

"There are lots worse things than being fat," Karma stated, coming back into the living room.

"Name three," Lisha commanded.

"Homelessness, racism, homophobia—"

"Come on, Mom, just call me," Chelsea urged, staring at the phone.

"She said she'll call, she'll call," Karma said, eating the last pretzel.

The phone rang.

"See?" Karma shrugged. "I'm psychic."

"I'm putting her on the speakerphone,"

Chelsea decided. "I need moral support. She picked up the receiver. "Hello?"

Karma listened while she opened the freezer. Yes! There was some coffee ice cream. She took out the container and got a spoon.

"Hello," Chelsea's mother said in her soft, genteel Southern voice.

"I've been really worried about you, Mom," Chelsea told her.

"I've been worried about you, too," Mrs. Jennings admitted.

"Well, then why didn't you return any of my phone calls?"

"This has been very difficult for me, Chelsea," her mother said.

"It hasn't exactly been a piece of cake for me, Mom."

Her mother sighed. "I knew that working for that tacky television program would not come to any good."

Chelsea shared a look with Karma.

Hang in there, Karma mouthed at her friend.

"Mom, I didn't plan for this to happen," Chelsea explained. "I didn't want it to happen—"

"Maybe you did, Chelsea," her mother cut in.

"I didn't!"

"You could never just leave it alone," her mother continued, her voice filled with stress. "You badgered me."

Karma stopped eating the coffee ice cream as

she watched, horrified, while Chelsea's eyes filled with tears.

"You want me to talk to her?" she offered.

"Or me," Lisha said, sitting up on the couch. "She knows me. I could explain."

Chelsea shook her head no. "Mom," she said into the speakerphone, "that is not fair."

Her mother was silent.

"You can't change the past by pretending it didn't happen," Chelsea went on. "Can't you see that?"

Silence.

"Mama? Are you there?"

"I'm here," her mother finally said. "Well, what's done is done. You can't put back spilled milk."

"No, you can't. What's going on with your job?"

"The principal gave me a short leave of absence. With pay."

"Well, that's good." Chelsea sighed. "Is the media leaving you alone?"

"For a while they were everywhere," Mrs. Jennings said. "I stayed with friends from church. It's pretty much over now."

"Well, that's great!" Chelsea exclaimed.

"It is," her mother agreed. "People still look at me at Kroger when I shop, though. And my summer students whisper about me behind their hands. They think I don't know, but I do."

"I'm sorry, Mom."

"Maybe you should just come home,

130

Chelsea," her mother said. "Wouldn't that be better?"

"No, it wouldn't."

"Remember what I told you before you left home?" Mrs. Jennings continued. "That if you lay down with dogs, you were going to get fleas?"

Chelsea closed her eyes. "I remember, Mom."

"Well, I guess you can see now that I was right."

"Right, Mom," Chelsea said. It was clear to Karma that she was too weary to argue. "Mom, what would you think if someone wanted to pay me to write a book?"

"You always did excel at creative writing, Chelsea."

"Well, it wouldn't exactly be fiction," Chelsea explained. "It would be . . . it would be the story of my life. Kind of."

Silence.

"Mom?" Chelsea called. "Say something."

"A publisher has offered you money to write about our family?" her mother said, her voice tight. "Is that it?"

"Yes," Chelsea admitted. "It's a lot of money, Mama."

"I don't care how much money it is," her mother said.

"But it's—"

"I don't care," her mother insisted. "And I can't believe you would even consider such a thing."

"But Mama—"

"Do you know what my mother used to say to me, may she rest in peace?" Mrs. Jennings asked. "She said a real lady only appeared in the newspaper three times in her life: when she was born, when she got married, and when she died."

Chelsea looked at Karma. Karma put down the ice cream and went to sit by her. She took Chelsea's hand.

"Now," Chelsea's mother continued, "how do you think my dear, departed mother would feel about you taking money to write about the tragedies of our family?"

"She wouldn't like it," Chelsea admitted.

"I raised you up to be a certain kind of person," Mrs. Jennings said. "You look into your heart, Chelsea, and I think you'll find the answer to your question."

"It's millions of dollars, Mama," Chelsea said quietly.

"Millions?"

"Millions," Chelsea confirmed.

"All I have to say is that is a sad commentary on the state that this country is in," Mrs. Jennings declared. "I think you should pray about this."

"I will," Chelsea replied.

"You're a good girl," Mrs. Jennings said, her voice softening. "I know this hasn't been easy for you."

"No, it hasn't," Chelsea agreed, her voice choking with emotion.

"Are you sure you don't want to come home, honey?"

"No, Mom," Chelsea answered. "I'm okay. I love you, Mama."

"I love you, too, honey," her mother said. "I'll call you soon some night after the rates change. And Chelsea?"

"What, Mom?"

"Remember what I said about the book."

Chelsea said good-bye and hung up the phone.

"At least you talked to her." Karma sighed.

Chelsea lay down on the rug and stared up at the ceiling. "She doesn't want me to do the book."

"You didn't expect her to, did you?" Lisha asked.

Chelsea shrugged. "I guess not."

"Anyway, you have to do what's right for you, not what's right for her," Lisha added.

Chelsea sat up. "But I can't just disregard her feelings! She's my mother. And it's *her* life, too."

"You should talk to her about it again," Karma counseled. "As your agent, it seems to me that—"

Their intercom buzzer went off.

"Now who could that be?" Karma mused. She scrambled up and went to the intercom box. "Yeah?"

Unintelligible mumbles and static.

"Yeah, sure, Antoine," Karma called back down. "Whatever."

"I'm not sure I like this new carefree attitude about letting people in," Chelsea opined.

"Hey, live dangerously," Lisha said.

Someone knocked on the door. Karma went to peer through the peephole. "It's Demetrius!"

Lisha looked at Chelsea and smiled. "And here you thought it was a crazed psycho."

Karma looked down at herself. She had on cutoffs and an old gray T-shirt. Her hair was up in a messy ponytail and she wasn't wearing any makeup. "I can't let him see me like this!" she yelped.

"Oh, give it a rest." Lisha walked around Karma to open the door. "You look cute."

"Hi, Your Studliness," she announced as she opened the door.

"Lish, I really don't like that nickname," Demetrius said.

Yeah, he likes Tree better, Karma thought.

"Hi," she said brightly. "What brings you here?"

Demetrius laughed. "You."

"Thanks," Karma said. "But we have a phone."

"I tried to call," Demetrius explained. "I kept getting a busy signal."

"We have call waiting," Lisha reminded him.

"Better get it checked, then," Demetrius said.

"I'm glad you're here," Karma told him. "You

want a beverage? We've got water and coffee. No one shopped."

"No, I'm fine." Demetrius put his arms around her. "I missed you."

"You just saw me at work today," Karma said, grinning up at him. "And you *definitely* saw me until early this morning, too." She stood on her tiptoes and Demetrius kissed her.

"Uh, excuse me, but could you two take this show into the bedroom?" Lisha asked.

"Sure," Karma said. She took Demetrius by the hand and led him into her room, then she shut the door.

"She has something against kissing?" Demetrius asked.

"I think she's romantically confused right now," Karma said, sitting on her bed.

Demetrius sat next to her. "She's seeing Alan, right?"

"But she's lusting after Sky," Karma explained. "She always has."

"So why isn't she with Sky, then?"

"You think I understand Lisha?" Karma asked. "I barely understand myself." She moved closer to him and kissed him softly. "You have the greatest lips. Did I ever mention that?"

"Not that I recall."

"Well, you do," Karma told him. "Really soft. Cushiony. Perfect." She kissed him again. "So, what did you do tonight?"

"I went to hear a lecture on Greek politics up at Columbia with my brother," Demetrius said.

"It must be great to have a brother you can hang out with," Karma said with a sigh.

"It is." He paused. "Alex and I were walking across campus to get to the lecture hall, and I saw Janelle."

Karma got a funny feeling in her stomach. "You did?"

Demetrius nodded. "It was so strange. The two of you are so identical—"

"I know—"

"For a moment I thought it was you. But then I realized she was wearing chinos and a white cotton shirt, and I knew you would never go out in public dressed like that. And I remembered you told me that Janelle is taking classes at Columbia."

"Yeah."

Demetrius stroked Karma's hair. "I'm sorry she doesn't want to know you, Karma. She's missing out on a truly great person."

Karma felt like crying, but she held back the tears. "Yeah, she is," she said.

"Maybe if you tried again—"

"Nah," Karma said, lying down on her back. "I'm pretty much through with trying, I think. She doesn't want to know me—fine. I don't want to know anyone who doesn't want to know me."

Demetrius lay down next to her. "You really amaze me."

"Yeah, I'm too wonderful, it's true," Karma whined.

Demetrius laughed. "And I admire the way you handled the situation with Mindy last night, too."

"Mindy who?" Karma asked, wide-eyed.

"Very funny." He tickled her ribs.

"She wants you back," Karma informed him.

"She doesn't—"

"She does," Karma insisted.

"Like I told you last night," Demetrius said patiently, "even if you're right, it doesn't matter."

"I don't know," Karma replied. "I bet she's a girl who usually gets what she wants."

"I bet she's not a girl who could have negotiated a multimillion-dollar book contract for her best friend," Demetrius pointed out.

Karma smiled. "That's true."

Demetrius studied her. "You know, you look cute without makeup."

"I look like I'm about ten years old."

"You look irresistible," he murmured, then leaned over and kissed her.

Karma put her arms around him and kissed him back. The kisses grew hotter. "Sit up," she told him, pushing him off of her.

"Why?"

"Just do it," Karma commanded.

Demetrius sat up.

Karma sat up, too. She put his hands over his head. Then she slowly lifted his T-shirt over his head and threw it into the corner. "You are a work of art," she said, staring at his hard, golden muscles.

"No," Demetrius said. "You are."

Gently, he lay Karma down and began kissing her again. She wrapped her arms around him, enjoying the smooth, taut feel of his skin.

"Karma," he groaned. Lifting the bottom of her T-shirt, he leaned down to kiss her stomach. Then slowly he began to inch the T-shirt upward, higher and higher. . . .

Dimly, Karma was aware that the phone was ringing, but she didn't care. All she cared about was Demetrius, and the feeling of being in his arms, and—

Someone was knocking on her door.

"Go away," Karma ordered.

"I'm sorry to bother you," Chelsea said.

"She said go away!" Demetrius called.

"It's the phone." Chelsea raised her voice. "It's Mrs. Cho. She said it's an emergency."

"Ignore her," Demetrius said, burying his face in Karma's hair.

"She probably wants to take me to lunch again," Karma said. "Some emergency."

She rolled over and snatched up the extension of the phone by her bed. "Hello?"

"Karma, it's Muriel Cho."

"I'm kind of busy, Mrs. Cho," Karma said. "My friend said this is an emergency?"

"It is," Mrs. Cho said. "There's been a terrible accident. It's Janelle."

10

"Janelle?" Karma repeated, clutching the phone hard in her hands. "What happened?"

"There was a terrible accident," Mrs. Cho said, choking out the words. "Thank God I have your phone number. Thank God."

"What happened?" Karma asked fearfully. "Is Janelle . . . alive?"

Demetrius sat up and put his arm around her.

"Yes," Mrs. Cho said. "She's alive. I'm calling you from the emergency room, Columbia Presbyterian. Upper Upper West Side. Do you know where it is?"

"Yes."

"Then come right away," Mrs. Cho said. "Please."

"But what happened?" Karma asked again.

"Can't talk now, doctor's coming, just hurry, Karma, please hurry!"

Mrs. Cho hung up.

Karma sat with the phone in her hand, dumbfounded.

"Karma?" Demetrius asked softly.

"It's Janelle," Karma said, hanging up the phone. "She had some kind of an accident. That was her mother." She stood up, dazed.

"What happened?"

"She didn't tell me." She looked around for her shoes. "I have to go—"

"Where?"

"Columbia Presbyterian," Karma said. "Where are my shoes?"

Demetrius found them under the bed and handed them to her. She slipped them on. "My sister," she said, reaching for her purse. "Something happened to my sister." She looked at Demetrius vaguely. "I don't know when I'll be back."

He put his arms around her. "Do you really think I'd let you go there alone?"

Karma walked into the living room and quickly told a stunned Chelsea and Lisha everything she knew, and said she'd call them if she had any news, then she and Demetrius ran into the hallway and pressed the elevator button. When it seemed to take forever, they gave up and ran down the many flights of stairs to the street.

"Taxi!" Demetrius yelled, waving his arm.

For once, an available taxi pulled over quickly.

"Columbia Presbyterian," Karma said as they got in the backseat. "And please hurry."

"You want me to make hurry?" the cabdriver said to her. "Okay, we hurry."

He stepped on the gas and headed over to Riverside Drive. There, he turned north, dodging around cars and blowing through lights as they changed from green to yellow and then on to red. Buildings flew by so fast on Karma's right that she felt like she was on an amusement park ride. To her left, she could see the Hudson River, the many pleasure boats drifting along it.

Pleasure boats, she thought, her hands shaking with fear. *Life is so bizarre. One minute you can be so happy, and then something horrible can happen, and then—*

No. Don't think like that, she told herself. *Janelle is alive. Maybe it won't be that bad.*

But something deep in her heart told her it was bad. Very bad.

Streets flew by: 110th Street . . . 125th Street . . . 145th Street. And finally, the cab was at 168th Street, turning east.

And there were the imposing edifices of Columbia Presbyterian Hospital, one of the great hospitals of New York, and a huge sign that read EMERGENCY.

"The emergency room, please," Karma said.

"Okay," the cabbie said, and pulled his cab to

a screeching stop right in front of the emergency entrance. Karma pulled a twenty-dollar bill out of her wallet and thrust it at him.

"Keep it," she told him.

"Thanks," the cabbie said, but Karma and Demetrius were already out of the cab and running through the entrance.

"Listen," Demetrius said, "I'll find the cafeteria and get some coffee. Come get me when you've got some news."

"No." Karma grabbed his arm. "I need—"

"They don't need to meet me now," Demetrius cut her off gently. "But you know I'm here, if you need me." He followed the sign that directed visitors to the hospital cafeteria.

When she entered the emergency-room waiting area, Karma saw Mr. and Mrs. Cho, Henry with his arm around a weary-looking Muriel, sitting side by side on some uncomfortable-looking orange plastic seats that could have been taken from a bus station.

She ran up to them.

"I came as fast as I could," she practically sobbed. "What happened?"

Mrs. Cho started to speak, but her voice dissolved in tears.

"Janelle was hit by a cab crossing Broadway," Mr. Cho explained, his face a mask of pain.

"Oh, God," Karma breathed.

"It's very serious," Mr. Cho added, tears in his eyes.

"Oh, God, I'm so sorry," Karma said, reaching

142

for their hands. "But she's . . . I mean, she could—"

I can't bring myself to ask if they expect her to live, she thought. *I just can't.*

"Where is she now?" Karma continued.

"She's getting an MRI," Mr. Cho explained. "They suspect internal bleeding."

Mrs. Cho began to cry softly. "My baby."

Then a thought hit Karma. A terrifying thought. And her hand flew to her mouth. "Her kidney!"

Oh no, Karma thought quickly. *I just totally, completely ruined it. Muriel made me promise her that I would never, ever say anything about how she called me, and how she met me, and how she told me about Janelle's kidney. And now I said it first. Which means that Mr. Cho now knows that . . . I am such an idiot.*

"Karma," Mr. Cho said gently, "Muriel told me everything. It doesn't matter now."

"Nothing matters," Mrs. Cho sobbed, "if God will just let my child live."

"We're glad you're here, Karma," Mr. Cho added, his eyes filling with tears again.

"I'm glad I'm here, too," Karma told them. She sat down next to them. "In fact, I'm honored that you called me."

Mrs. Cho nodded and reached for her hand again.

They are in so much pain, Karma thought. *What if it were my parents, and I was the one in there, fighting for my life?*

143

"Is there anything at all I can do to help you?" she asked.

Mr. and Mrs. Cho exchanged an odd look.

"There is something," Mrs. Cho began slowly.

"Tell me," Karma urged. "I want to help."

Mrs. Cho looked down at her hands. "It's hard to ask. I know Janelle wasn't very interested in being your friend."

"She's still my twin sister," Karma reminded them.

"Identical twin," Mr. Cho said. "Identical. Do you know what that means?"

"It means we're the same, except for our personalities," Karma said. "It means . . . oh."

No, she thought. *Don't ask me what I think you're about to ask me.*

"It might be her kidney, they said," Muriel said gently. "She only has one kidney."

"A person cannot live without a working kidney," Mr. Cho added, "unless they are on a dialysis machine. And even then, the prognosis is very grim."

"You would be a perfect genetic match to Janelle," Mrs. Cho said.

They want my kidney.

She'd have one kidney, and I'd have one kidney.

But she was such a bitch to me.

Why in the world should I do it? Why?

"I'm so glad you're here," Karma said, running into her parents' open arms. She had been waiting in the cafeteria with Demetrius. Although she had called them right after the Chos told her Janelle's condition, it was a good hour's drive from their home on Long Island into the city, and then across town to the hospital.

And I called Lisha and Chelsea, too, and left a message for them to come, Karma thought. *I guess they went out after Demetrius and I left. I could really use my friends now. Really.*

Demetrius rose from the plastic chair he was sitting in and shook hands with Marty and Wendy. He had been out to Karma's parents' house a couple of times and already knew them.

They were dressed in their usual old-hippie clothes—Wendy in a long skirt and peasant blouse, Marty with his hair and beard scraggly, in drawstring pants and a long-sleeved T-shirt advertising some 1960s band, Moby Grape, whom Karma had heard of only through her dad's wardrobe.

"We got here as soon as we could," Wendy said, sitting down next to her daughter.

Marty sat, too, as did Demetrius. "What do you know so far?" Marty asked.

"A lot," Karma said. "They did an MRI. It is her kidney. A couple of ribs were shattered by the taxi, and they kind of floated back and lacerated her kidney. She's in surgery now—they're trying to stop the bleeding."

"Could she die?" Wendy asked, reaching for her daughter's hand.

"They don't think so," Demetrius said. "Which is about the only good news we've heard."

"Where are her parents?" Marty asked.

"With her."

"And they asked you if—"

"Yes," Karma affirmed. "They asked me if I'd be willing to donate one of my kidneys to her. Now. The doctors are waiting for me to decide. If I say yes, they'll do the transplant right away."

"She doesn't need a transplant to live right now," Demetrius explained. "But it would be a very bad situation for her. She'd have to have dialysis every day. And eventually she would still need the transplant."

"And you're her perfect match," Wendy said, squeezing her daughter's hand.

"Dr. Rhodes, Dr. Rhodes, second floor, stat," a voice announced on the intercom. Karma saw a weary-looking female intern in green scrubs, a stethoscope slung around her neck, get to her feet. "Dr. Rhodes, Dr. Susan Rhodes, Room 249, stat."

To Karma's left, a young woman sobbed in the arms of an older man. And next to them, an elderly woman with shaking hands ate a lonely meal of cottage cheese and crackers.

What a horrible, awful, depressing place this is, she thought. *I wish I was anywhere but here. Doing anything but this.*

At that moment Mr. and Mrs. Cho entered the cafeteria. They were looking in the other direction and didn't notice Karma.

"That's them," Karma said, cocking her head toward the couple.

Mr. Cho turned his head and saw Karma. She smiled at him. He nodded. Mrs. Cho nodded, too, then looked away.

It's like they're begging me with their eyes, Karma thought. *How did I ever get put in this position?*

"We should go be with them," Wendy said, getting up.

"No, Mom," Karma protested.

"But, Karma—"

"Not until I decide. Please. I can't face them until I decide."

"I'm going to meet them," Wendy announced, getting to her feet. "They're so . . . so sad."

Karma's mom walked over to the Chos, and Karma watched as her mother said a few words she couldn't hear. Mr. and Mrs. Cho nodded, and then Wendy Kushner returned.

"What did you say?" Karma asked.

"I said I was praying for their daughter," Wendy said simply. "I said we're all praying."

Karma buried her face in her hands. "I don't want to have to make this decision! It isn't fair!"

"Life so rarely is, honey," her father said gently.

"But Janelle was so mean to me! She didn't

147

even want to know me! Why would I risk my own life for her? Why?"

"Have you talked to the doctors yet, Karma?" Marty asked.

Karma nodded. She had talked with the doctors. She explained to her parents what they had told her, that there were going to be some tests she needed to have done before they could be sure she would be an eligible kidney donor, but those could be taken care of right away. Quickly.

And if the tests were all fine, the surgery could be performed right away.

"So, what do you think?" Marty asked.

"I think . . . I don't know," Karma wailed. Then, sighing deeply: "If it was any of you . . . or if it was Chelsea or Lisha . . . but it isn't."

"No, it isn't," her father agreed.

"Karma—" her mother began.

"I know what you're going to say, Mom," Karma interrupted. "Janelle is my sister." She paused before adding, "My only sister."

"Karma," her dad said to her, looking over at the Chos, "do you remember your Torah portion?"

"He means the part of the Torah I read for my bat mitzvah," Karma explained to Demetrius. "A bat mitzvah is—"

"I know what a bat mitzvah is," Demetrius said. "It's the ceremony you have where you

148

read from the Hebrew Bible when you turn thirteen, right?"

"Right," Karma agreed.

"My uncle José is married to Sheila Nussbaum, president of Temple Emmanuel in Flushing."

"You never told me that," Karma said in surprise.

Demetrius shrugged. "It never came up."

Marty turned back to his daughter. "So, do you remember your Torah portion, sweetie?"

"Dad, I don't need a religion lecture now—"

"I'm just asking you if you remember," Marty said.

"Yeah, of course I remember," Karma told him. "It was the Ten Commandments."

"Karma and her dad studied together," Wendy said proudly.

"Talk about tough." Karma rolled her eyes. "He was relentless."

"I wanted you to pay attention," Marty said mildly. "Even back then you wanted to look at the stock reports instead of paying attention."

"So, I was a business prodigy," Karma said defensively.

"Do you remember what the Jewish scholars said about breaking a commandment?" Marty asked.

"Dad—"

"Stay with me, honey," her father urged. "Everything worth knowing in life cannot be found in *Business Week*. Do you remember?"

"Yeah," Karma recalled. "You must break a commandment to save a life."

"That's right." Marty beamed at his daughter with pride. "You remembered."

"Maybe I paid more attention than you thought," Karma said reluctantly.

"You *must* break a commandment if it means you will be saving a life," Marty repeated, nodding. "Saving a life is the most important thing. It's *pekuach nefesh,* in Hebrew. It's the best that a person can do."

"But she was such a bitch to me," Karma wailed.

Marty looked again at his daughter, and smiled. "If you're walking by the ocean, and you hear a person calling out in the surf because they're drowning, do you wait to see who the person is before you go in to rescue him?"

Karma was silent for a moment. "I see your point," she finally said. "That doesn't mean I like your point. But I see it."

Marty patted her hand. "That's my girl."

"I thought you were an old hippie," Karma said to her dad.

"I'm an old *Jewish* hippie," he corrected, "and so is your mother. And the world could use a few more of us."

Karma looked from her father to her mother, and tears came to her eyes. She thought about how much she loved them.

Even if they are among the most fashion-

challenged human beings I have ever known in my life.

"Excuse me," Karma said, and she got to her feet.

She walked over to the Chos, who were huddled together over cups of tea.

"Mr. and Mrs. Cho?"

They looked up at her, their eyes pools of naked hope, naked need.

"You've decided?" Mr. Cho said.

"I want you to know," Karma told them, "that I have the best mother and father in the world."

They nodded, their hands wrapped around their teacups.

"And I want you to know something else," Karma said.

They just stared at her. Mrs. Cho's lower lip was trembling.

Karma took a deep breath.

"I'll do it."

11

"**Y**ou're sure?" Demetrius asked, holding Karma's hand tight.

"No," Karma retorted. "What do I look like, some kind of bizarre Korean-Jewish saint? I'm not sure about anything. But I'm going to do it, anyway."

It was two hours later, and Karma was in a private room on the same floor as Janelle. She had gone through all the necessary tests to ascertain if she could donate a kidney to Janelle.

She could. She would.

She looked at the clock on the wall.

In a half hour I'm going to get wheeled in to major surgery, she thought. *They're going to remove my kidney. Which means that if anything ever happens to the one kidney I'll have left, I will be in big, big trouble.*

No, I can't think about that now.

Her parents walked into the room. Her mother kissed her forehead.

"Don't treat me like I'm sick," Karma instructed. "I'm not sick."

"We know that," her father said, kissing her cheek.

"And can we talk to someone about this little garmento?" Karma groused, gingerly holding up a pinch of the material of her hospital gown. "Wearing this would prevent anyone from getting well. It's so depressing!"

"We'll get your roommates to bring you some other nightgowns," Wendy assured her.

"I wonder where they are," Demetrius remarked. "You called and left a message a long time ago."

Maybe it didn't seem important to them, Karma thought. *Maybe they just couldn't be bothered. Which would mean that I love them a lot more than they love me.*

Ouch.

"I'm gonna have a scar, you know," Karma told Demetrius. "Probably a really yucky one. You should know that."

"Do you really think I care?" he asked.

"Well, I care, then." Karma pouted. "Gawd, I just thought of something. What if I get fired from *Trash* because of this?"

"They're not going to fire you because you had emergency surgery to save your sister's life," her father said patiently. "It's both illegal and unethical."

"Trash doesn't care about legal and ethical," Karma shot right back.

"They won't fire you," Demetrius said. "Jazz might want to show the surgery on *Trash*, of course—"

"Oh, that's *so* funny," Karma whined. She plucked at the sheet that covered her legs. "I don't mind admitting that I'm a little bit . . . nervous. Okay, I'm real nervous."

"It's going to be okay, honey," her mother said soothingly, smoothing the hair off Karma's forehead.

"You don't know that," Karma snapped.

Wendy smiled sadly. "You're right. I don't. I was saying a soothing mother-type thing."

"I've heard that hospital food is the worst," Karma said. "So you all have to promise to bring me junk food."

"We promise," Demetrius said solemnly.

Karma looked at the clock again. "Twenty minutes to show time," she noted.

A nurse came into the room. She was African-American, heavyset, with her hair in tiny braids fastened with multicolored beads.

"How you doing?" she said warmly. "I'm Mrs. Eddings."

"Karma Kushner," Karma said. "President and CEO of the Kushner Agency."

Her parents looked at her as if she were crazy.

"It's a long story," Karma murmured.

155

The nurse smiled as she took Karma's pulse. "You look awfully young to have that position."

"I'm a prodigy," Karma explained.

"So, you all set to rock and roll?" the nurse asked.

"Surgery is not rock and roll," Karma corrected.

"Just an expression," Mrs. Eddings said. "Your pulse is fine."

"I know," Karma said nervously. "I'm fine. I'm not the one who needs the surgery. But I'm crazy enough to be having it, anyway."

"I need to give you a shot," Mrs. Eddings said. "It will help you relax. Then we'll finish your prep, and then we'll wheel you down to surgery."

Surgery. Gulp.

"Uh, maybe I should rethink all of this," Karma said, her voice small.

"It's your decision," her father said. "You don't have to do this."

"Oh, yeah, right," Karma snorted. "Like you wouldn't be disappointed in me for the rest of my life."

"Karma." Marty took her hand, "I will love you no matter what."

"But you think I should do it," Karma said.

"I think you should listen to your heart." He smiled down at her.

Karma sighed. "Why do I have to have such spiritual parents? Can you answer me that?"

Mrs. Eddings laughed. "I say that about my father all the time. He's a Baptist preacher. I'll be right back." She bustled out of the room.

Karma looked at the clock again.

"I guess my friends aren't coming," she said, trying to keep the disappointment out of her voice.

"They must not have gotten your message," her mother reasoned.

"Yeah, I guess," Karma muttered. "It's okay. I mean, it's not like it's so important or anything—"

Her eyes filled with tears.

"Karma?"

She looked up.

Standing at the door was Chelsea.

The door opened wider.

There was Lisha. And Nick. And Alan. And Sky.

They all came into the room.

"It took you guys long enough!" Karma whined, sniffling back her tears.

"We just got your message," Chelsea said as the whole gang gathered around Karma. "We went to a movie. And then we went for pizza—"

"We came over here as soon as we heard," Alan said.

"We're just going to sneak out for a few minutes before they kick all of us out," Wendy told

Karma, reaching for her husband's hand. "We'll be back."

"I sweet-talked that nurse with the cool braids to let us in," Nick explained.

"Mrs. Eddings," Karma said, smiling.

"You're giving Janelle your kidney?" Lisha asked.

Karma nodded.

"You're a better woman than I am," Lisha told her. "I don't think I could do it."

"You'd be surprised what you can do," Karma said softly.

"We'll stay here all through the surgery," Chelsea promised, taking Karma's hand.

"I think it takes a while," Karma said.

"It doesn't matter," Sky reassured her. "If you're here, we're here."

"What about work?" Karma asked.

"What about it?" Lisha asked back. "Some things are more important."

Tears filled Karma's eyes. "Thanks. Really. I . . . it means a lot to me that you guys are all here. I feel like . . . well, I guess I feel more like you're my family than Janelle is."

"That's good to know, in case I need any spare body parts from you," Sky quipped.

"I've been thinking, Karma," Chelsea began slowly. "There's something I need to tell you."

"Don't make any big confessions," Karma begged. "I'm having surgery, I'm not dying."

"It isn't a confession," Chelsea said. "It's

just . . . something I figured out. But I think you're going to be mad at me."

"Uh-oh," Karma groaned. "You're not doing the book."

"Right," Chelsea agreed. "I'm not. My mom is the only family I have. And I can't put her through that. And . . . well, I can't get out of my mind what Billy Slocum said. It *would* be blood money. It isn't right to profit from that kind of horrible tragedy."

"I think she's crazy," Lisha said bluntly.

"I don't know what I think," Karma admitted. "It would have been nice to wake up from this little surgery knowing I was minus a kidney but plus more than two hundred grand."

"I'm sorry," Chelsea told her. "I feel like I've let you down."

"Nah," Karma said. "The Kushner Agency will just have to find another really big client. Fast."

"Okay, Miss Kushner," Mrs. Eddings called, coming back into the room. "Ready for your shot?"

"No," Karma declared.

"Well, you take the shot and I'll pretend I didn't see six people visiting in here at the same time, how's that?"

She swabbed Karma's arm and stuck in the needle quickly. "All done." She turned to Karma's friends. "Finish up your visit, children. Miss Kushner is going for a ride in five." She left the room.

"I'm scared," Karma whispered, gulping hard.

Demetrius took her hand. "I love you, Karma," he said softly.

"We all love you," Chelsea said.

"So . . . I guess I'll see all of you when I wake up, huh?" Karma asked.

"Count on it," Alan promised.

One by one they all kissed her good-bye.

Her parents came in and did the same.

And then, Karma was alone.

I'm doing the right thing, she told herself. *And I'm going to come out of this fine. And I will have done this really, really cool thing for another person, even if that person kind of seems to hate my guts.*

One tear traveled down her cheek.

Dear God, she prayed. *I'm so scared.*

"Now what?" Sky asked as they all went to sit in the waiting area that was nearest to surgery.

"We wait," Mr. Kushner said.

"It will be hours," his wife added. "If you guys want to go, we'll call you."

"Not a chance." Lisha folded her arms.

"I know it's silly," Chelsea said, "but I feel like Karma will be fine, as long as we're all here."

Karma's mother hugged Chelsea close. "That's a lovely thing to say."

Chelsea sat.

A doctor emerged from one of the doors to surgery and looked around, his eyes finally lighting on a middle-aged couple sitting near the group. They hurried over to him.

"Your son is fine," he told them. "They're wheeling him into the recovery room now."

"In just a few hours that's what we'll be hearing," Marty said.

"Right," Wendy agreed. "And so will the Chos. I believe it with all my heart."

At that moment the Chos entered the waiting room. They walked over to Karma's parents.

"Your daughter is doing a wonderful thing," Mrs. Cho said tremulously. "I can't thank you enough—"

"Please, you've thanked us already." Wendy helped Muriel into a seat. "Both girls are going to be fine."

"After this, I can't believe that they won't become friends," Mr. Cho said.

"Sisters, even," Marty added. "That would be nice."

"Can I get any of you anything?" Chelsea asked them. "Coffee? A cold drink?"

"No, nothing, thank you." Mrs. Cho tried to smile as she unclenched and unclenched her hands.

"Waiting is hard," Chelsea told her. She walked back over to her friends. "Isn't it kind

161

of odd that none of Janelle's friends are here?"

"Maybe her parents didn't call anyone," Demetrius said.

"Or maybe Janelle is as nasty to everyone as she is to Karma," Lisha suggested. "In which case, she doesn't have any friends."

"We're definitely throwing Karma a party as soon as she's better," Chelsea decided.

"Absolutely," Nick agreed, putting his arm around her. "Belch can be the entertainment."

"Belch can get locked up in the bedroom," Chelsea said, laughing.

A tall, slender, balding young doctor rushed into the waiting area. His eyes scanned the group. Then he walked over to Karma's parents. "Mr. and Mrs. Kushner?"

They stood up.

"I'm Dr. Tucci, part of the team operating on your daughter, Karma."

Karma's friends overheard, and gathered around. The Chos did, too.

"What is it?" Wendy asked nervously. "Why are you out here? Isn't the surgery about to begin?"

"We just gave her the anesthesia," Dr. Tucci said. "I'm afraid . . . she's had a very bad reaction to it."

Marty grabbed the doctor's hand. "What do you mean, a bad reaction?"

"She's . . . I'm sorry, sir. But it's very grave."

"But . . . that can't be." Marty struggled to

control his voice. "I mean, you didn't even start yet—"

"I'm sorry, sir," the young doctor said. "They're in there doing everything they can right now."

"Are you saying that . . . Karma could die?" Chelsea asked, her voice hushed, horrified.

"Yes," the doctor admitted. "She could die."

THE TRASH CAN

Hey Readers,

Jeff here—Cherie is locked in her office doing a rewrite on her latest play. She sends you her love, lots of hugs and kisses and all that. The woman is so sentimental. But, hey, that's one of the reasons I fell in love with her. Don't tell her I said so.

We've been hearing a lot of this from you guys lately: Cherie and Jeff, we are totally into *Trash*. But those cliffhangers are making us crazy!

Yeah, we're merciless, I know. But hey, eventually you do find out how every cliffhanger ends, right? Which one has been your favorite so far?

The next *Trash* out is *Truth or Scare*. What's it about? Well, here's a hint. Maybe Harley is dead. And maybe he isn't. And maybe he left Lisha with something more than bad memories.

The biggest question we get asked is how we can write together without killing each other. We just seem to have some kind of mind-meld when it comes to these books. We still hardly ever argue about plots, or even about lines of dialogue. We even have the same favorite character. Can you guess who it is? And who is your fave, by the by?

Update: During the past few months, Cherie finished another new play *Zink: The Myth. The Legend. The Zebra.* It's about a young girl who has leukemia, and although that sounds depressing, it really isn't. The world premiere will be in Milwaukee in November of 1997.

Hope you'll get to see it, or one of her other plays, sometime soon. They're being done all over the country.

Wanna write to us? It's Jeff & Cherie, PO Box 150326, Nashville, TN 37215. All mail gets answered, but send a SASE to speed your reply. E-mail us at: authorchik@aol.com.

Remember, if you're even gonna be in Nashville, let us know ahead of time, and if we're in town, we'll take you to lunch. Your parents have to sit at another table, or they can pick you up later. We love to meet our readers.

Thanks for sharing your thoughts, ideas, hopes and dreams with us. We're honored. Love ya! Mean it!

How TRASHy it is!

Jeff

Hey, Cherie and Jeff!

I am a fifteen-year-old guy, and I really like your books. You probably don't get a lot of mail from guys, right? I used to read horror, but now it's like same old, same old. I'd rather read about real life. One thing about the two *Trash* books I've read is that the guys seem real to me. I wonder if your girl readers could answer a question for me. What is most important to a girl: looks, money or brains? And could you print their answers? Also, girls—please don't say brains just because you think it's the right thing to say. Thanks! I love your books.

Billy Appel
Memphis, Tennessee

Hey, Billy!

Actually, we've been getting more and more mail from guys lately. So, here's your letter, and I invite all you girls out there to write in and answer Billy's question. We'll print the best answers in a future *Trash*!

Jeff

Hey, Cherie!

I want to join your fan club. Hope it's still open. Anyway, as to the first letter you got from me, the name on it is just a pen name. Pen names are not just for published authors! My real name is Pia. I love reading your books.

Pia Reyes
Irvine, California

Hey, Pia!

So, you've got a pen name of your own? Too cool. Anyone else out there have a pen name? Making up a name for yourself, or for characters in a play or novel is incredibly fun. So, do you think the names Chelsea, Karma, and Lisha are right for the heroines of *Trash*? Hey, send us ideas for a great guy's name. He's hot, evil, and in a future *Trash*. He's determined to come between Chelsea and Nick!

Jeff

Hey, Cherie!

I just saw you have an e-mail address, and I wanted to tell you I totally love all your books.

I've read them all, including the new *Trash* series. I think *Trash* is your best series other than *Sunset Island*. It's got great cliffhanger endings, and I am totally eager for the next book to come out. I think you're an awsome writer.

LaurEeyore@aol.com
(via e-mail)

Hey, LaurEeyore!
It was great to get your e-mail. Now, we hope you're surprised to see it in print in a *Trash* book. We get lots of e-mail (authorchik@aol.com), and there is a huge group of our readers who are also key-pals to each other. We help you all meet each other. In addition to answering e-mail, we've got our own Web site now: http://www.geocities. com/soho/lofts/8955/cherie.htm/. Check it out! Thanks for writing.

Jeff